fiona dunbar

The Silk Sisters

PiNK
chameleon

ORCHARD BOOKS

Thanks to Christine Liu of MIT, for filling me in on all those fascinating technical facts about Smart clothing, just so I could go off and make it all up anyway. Thanks also to Judith Goodman and Mohammed Ashraf, for their advice. Thanks once again to Siobhan Dowd for actually being prepared to read the thing even after all my agonising down the phone, and also to Lee Weatherly for listening to similar rants. And thanks as ever to my cousin Mat, and to Helena xxx.

ORCHARD BOOKS
338 Euston Road, London NW1 3BH
Orchard Books Australia
Level 17/207 Kent Street, Sydney NSW 2000

ISBN 978 1 84616 230 5

A paperback original
First published in 2007
Text copyright © Fiona Dunbar
The right of Fiona Dunbar to be identified as the author of this work has been asserted by her in accordance with the Copyright, Designs and Patents Act, 1988.

12

Printed in Great Britain.

The paper and board used in this paperback are natural recyclable products made from wood grown in sustainable forests. The manufacturing processes conform to the environmental regulations of the country of origin.

Orchard Books is a division of Hachette Children's Books, an Hachette UK company.
www.hachette.co.uk

"Fashion is what one wears oneself; what is unfashionable is what other people wear."

Oscar Wilde

Contents

A Note From The Author

It may not seem possible to you right now, but there will come a time when JEANS are no longer the thing that everyone wears. I have a confession to make: I don't like jeans much. For years, I resisted: I didn't wear jeans, ever. Eventually I had to give in, because they were all you could get in the shops. But any time I'm in a place where there are a lot of people, like a shopping centre or an airport, I look out upon that vast ocean of washed-out, bleached-out, saggy-bottomed, fraying-bottomed, boot-cut, classic-cut, skinny-fit, relaxed-fit denim and I find it depressing. Oh look, it's the Blue Rinse Brigade again.

I don't know in what year this story takes place, but I can tell you one thing: the whole jeans thing will have passed. Instead, people will be wearing SLANTS. Slants will have all the benefits of jeans; comfortable, better-looking as they get older...even, for some, the ability to make a flabby bottom look more compact. Originally 'slouch pants' (the name soon gets abbreviated), they will be a dark purply-red and made from a kind of fabric originally devised for Mars miners. So when you read about someone in this story wearing 'slants' you'll know what I'm talking about.

Chapter 1
Poker Bute Hall

Arthur Clarkson was not having a good day; you could tell this because he had turned a very murky dark green all over. Given that he'd had to spend the last few hours in Rorie's pocket, this was hardly surprising.

Elsie leaned over and stroked the pet chameleon's head. 'Oh Arthur, not too long now, OK?'

Arthur Clarkson just turned murkier. His throat quivered and his eyes – those crazy eyes like two rotating volcanoes – swivelled independently, anxiously trying to make sense of it all.

Rorie gazed at him pitifully. 'Shush, Elsie,' she whispered to her little sister. 'He's not in the mood, look.' He was not a sociable lizard at the best of times, and these were anything but the best of times. Of course, it *was* rather dark in Rorie's pocket, and like all chameleons, Arthur Clarkson – who got his name from a rather odd-looking reclusive genius known to the family – tended to blend in with his surroundings. But Rorie had only seen him this dark once before, and that was when he'd got lost and was being taunted by the neighbour's cat. Poor thing took weeks to get over that. Eventually they knew he was fine when his markings began, once again, to proclaim his wellbeing in rainbow hues. Rorie had always thought it must be rather wonderful to be able to change colour like that according to your mood.

'Quick, hide him,' hissed Elsie, 'they're coming back'.

Rorie swiftly pocketed the chameleon again, as the door opened and in walked Uncle Harris and Aunt Irmine. Just seeing them churned Rorie's stomach; if she were a chameleon she would have been bog-coloured too.

Uncle Harris was a tall, imposing man, with an angry fist of a face that seemed to be composed entirely of tightly wrought sinew. On the front of it sat a nose-and-moustache arrangement two sizes too big. On the sides, two perfectly round, shiny purple ears perched exactly at ninety degrees, like handles. 'Time to go,' he announced brusquely.

'Girls,' added Aunt Irmine, the slight fluttering of her tiny hand indicating that one must stand to attention. She really was the oddest shape, thought Rorie, starting out bulky at the top, and tapering down to improbably small hands and feet. Her hulking shoulders seemed intended for a rugby player, and her heavy unibosom lolloped from side to side under her shapeless sweater as she walked. She had no neck to speak of, and her formidable bulldog jaw thrust itself forward defiantly.

The girls stood up; Uncle Harris grimaced, clearly disenchanted with their appearance. 'Now then; as you know, your father and I have never really seen eye-to-eye on...matters.'

Rorie and Elsie glanced at each other at this reference to their father. *Oh Dad! Come back, Dad...*

Uncle Harris wagged a long, sinuous finger. 'Now don't you forget! Irmine and I' – he pronounced the name "Er-*mine*" – 'are taking you in out of the goodness of our hearts.'

'Out of the goodness of our hearts,' added Aunt Irmine.

'So there's to be no trouble, understand?'

'Yes, Uncle Harris.'

'Of course, you'll have to attend our school.'

Rorie's jaw fell open. 'We'll have to – *what*?'

'It's the only way,' insisted Aunt Irmine, shaking her bulldog head in a falsely-apologetic-but-really-bossy way.

'OWWWW!!' cried Elsie, bursting into tears.

Rorie put her arm around her, while trying hard to stop herself from doing the same. Having both your parents disappear suddenly was quite bad enough, without having to move to some boarding school full of strangers as well. Even when your uncle's the head teacher and your aunt's the deputy – no, *especially* then. Oh, why did he have to be the *only* family member available to take care of them? If only Granny were still alive, and Great-Grandma not simply too old...If only Mum had some family, apart from a sister in Australia with four young kids. If only, if only...

If only Mum and Dad would come back.

'I said, there's to be *no trouble*,' repeated Uncle Harris. 'Now, it will be different from *your* school, no question about that. At Poker Bute Hall, we instil a real sense of discipline, right from the start. And just because we're related, you needn't expect any sort of preferential treatment.'

Aunt Irmine nodded. 'What's sauce for the goose is sauce for the gander.'

Elsie broke off from her sobbing. 'What's a gander?'

Aunt Irmine and Uncle Harris exchanged pitiful glances. 'It's a male goose,' explained Aunt Irmine.

'But I don't eat goose!' exclaimed Elsie, bursting into tears again. 'And I only like *tomato* sauce!'

'Ssh!' said Rorie, comforting her. 'You won't have to eat goose, Elsie.' She felt Arthur Clarkson squirm in her pocket, which seemed to draw Uncle Harris's attention.

She froze, then realised her uncle was actually looking at some papers on the table.

He picked them up. 'Right then; come along. I take it you returned that lizard of yours to the pet shop, as you were instructed?'

'He's a chameleon,' corrected Elsie.

Uncle Harris turned his beady-eyed frown on her. 'I beg your pardon?'

'Arthur Clarkson,' said Elsie. 'He's a *chameleon*. Not just any old lizard.'

Rorie blushed. Elsie was incredibly forthright for a seven-year-old.

Uncle Harris stepped forward and thrust his angry-fist face at the girls, casting them into heavy shadow. 'But this *chameleon*,' he uttered in a low, menacing voice, almost a whisper, '…is gone now, am I correct?'

'Yes', chorused the two sisters, nodding furiously.

Reluctantly, they followed their aunt and uncle outside. Uncle Harris placed his forefinger on the car's ID pad, and they got in. Rorie barely knew him, but already he had set her teeth on edge – especially with that remark about 'not seeing eye to eye' with Dad. As if there were something *superior* about his own point of view! *He's just jealous*, thought Rorie. Jealous of Dad's brilliant, sparkling genius.

'Good afternoon,' said the velvety female voice of the car, once they were seated. 'Please state driver's name.'

'Harris Silk.'

The car hummed in response, and they drove off.

It was one of those bright, glistening days that could almost make you feel that everything is right with the world. Almost…but not for Rorie, not today. No amount of sunshine could make up for the fact that her life had been turned upside down overnight. She still found it completely incomprehensible that their parents were…gone. Vanished. That just didn't *happen*.

Chapter 2
The Inventor

As they drove away from their home, Rorie's imagination turned every pedestrian she saw into Mum or Dad. Her mind drifted back to Sunday evening. It had started out in such a familiar, mundane way, with Elsie complaining that Dad never seemed to have dinner with the rest of the family any more.

Dishing out the noodle soup, Mum had promised – for the umpteenth time – that 'any day now', they were in for a big surprise. Rorie remembered how tired Mum had looked; she had been working as hard as Dad, staying up well into the night. Her eyes were just like Rorie's own – oriental and startlingly pale contrasting with dark lashes and high ink-black brows – but in Mum's case the brows had thinned out, and there were dark circles under her eyes.

For weeks, Elsie had been desperate to know what

the mystery project was. She had tried to break into the lab, but was foiled by Dad's complex range of security devices. So she had resorted to attempts to distract him with a range of 'emergencies', from deliberately flooding the toilet to pretending Arthur Clarkson was having a heart attack; so far none of them had worked. All Elsie knew was that the project was something to do with *clothes*, and this made it all the more tantalising; Elsie was passionate about clothes the way that dolphins are passionate about water. Dressing up was, as Rorie would say, Elsie's reason for existing.

There were two things about Elsie that drove Rorie up the wall: one, she never could keep a secret; and two, she told tall tales all the time. In a way this was just as well, because any time Elsie let slip something she wasn't supposed to, Rorie could just put it down to Elsie's fibbing. As it was, most people didn't actually believe their dad was an inventor. 'Don't be daft, you don't get inventors any more,' they'd say. 'Inventors' belonged to the dusty old era when people still relied on vehicles with petrol engines and clunky old computers with a dozen cables sprouting out the back. The idea of 'inventors' in the hydrogen age seemed quaint. But Elsie would point to everything from an MPJ to a force-field crash helmet and say, 'My dad invented that, he did.' And sometimes it was true, but a lot of times it wasn't. And if she was caught out – like the time a smart-alecky friend pointed out that MPJs had been around 'since before your dad was even born!' – then she still found some way around it, claiming that her dad was really seventy years old, but only looked forty-two because he'd invented this amazing face cream that makes you look way younger than you really were. Elsie never, ever admitted she was lying.

In fact, it turned out that the MPJ, or Music-Playing Jacket, was an innovation that helped pave the way for Dad's Very Exciting Invention. Only moments after Elsie had complained about his absence, the sound of footsteps approached from the basement. Then Dad appeared at the door, in the same shabby slants and sweater he'd worn for the last three days, a wild, bleary-eyed grin on his face...

Elsie slid off her seat and clattered across the kitchen in her pink sparkly sling-backs. 'Are you fishit?' she asked, reverting to baby talk in her hurried excitement.

Dad scooped her up in his arms. 'I'm not only fishit, I'm going to *show* you what I've fishit!'

'Now?'

'Hmm,' said Dad, a joke frown on his face. 'Or we could book an appointment. Next Thursday any good for you?'

Elsie thumped him. 'Dad!'

Mum, suddenly energised, began jumping around like a toddler on a sugar rush. 'Yes! We did it, we did it...whoo-hoo!' She grabbed Dad by the arm. 'Come on Arran – I've been dying to tell the girls!'

They all hurtled down the stone stairs, Elsie stumbling in her sling-backs and nearly spraining her ankle.

'What is it?' cried Elsie, as they entered the lab.

'You'll see...'

Ever since she was little, Rorie had associated the lab's strange, acrid smell with great things. For all its stench, dust and appalling clutter, this felt like seeing inside the brain of a genius. She tingled with excitement.

'Just wait till you see these designs!' said Mum, as she disappeared behind the dressing screen.

'Designs for *what*?' shrieked Elsie.

'Shush,' said Rorie, nudging her as they took their seats. 'They'll show us if you'd just shut up for half a minute.'

'I'm not stopping them!' retorted Elsie. 'Hey, I bet it's a suit that makes you go invisibubble...is it, Dad? Is it a ninvisble suit?'

'Nope,' said Dad, his head briefly popping up from

behind the screen before continuing his hushed discussion with Mum.

Elsie twirled her hair and swung her feet impatiently, dropping a sling-back. 'Is i-i-t-t...' She struggled to get the shoe back on over her grubby sock. 'Is it something that does that thing like when you, you know, go away from one place and disappear completely and then you—'

'Teleportation,' said Rorie. 'Don't be a twit.'

'Oh! The movie's starting!' cried Elsie, as the three computer screens on the back wall suddenly flushed with colour, showing images of people in different outfits.

Dad reappeared, now smart and handsome in a charcoal grey suit; the girls applauded. 'So-called 'Smart' clothing – the thinfat jacket, the heart monitor vest, clothing that plays music, displays pictures – has become a part of everyday life,' he began. 'But until now, we've had to rely on electronic components woven into textiles, which means limited capabilities and lifespan. So I began to look at completely new ways of making Smart clothes...going back to nature!'

The screens showed a fish, a cat and a newly-hatched butterfly. 'New ways to advance thinfat technology...'

The fish puffed itself into a ball, the cat's fur fluffed up in hostility, the butterfly's wings became thin and rigid as they filled with blood.

'...And colour-changing technology.'

Now an octopus, a zebrafish and a chameleon appeared on the screens.

'Arthur Clarkson!' exclaimed Elsie.

'Lols?' called Dad, and Mum emerged, flushed with excitement in knee-length black boots and a plain white dress. 'What sort of day is it today?'

'Hmm,' thought Mum. 'I'd say it was a RED day...' The dress instantly turned red.

Both girls gasped in admiration.

'...With PURPLE POLKA DOTS,' Mum added: the polka dots appeared. 'No, SMALLER... SMALLER...GOOD.' The pattern on the dress altered according to every verbal instruction.

'Once the dress is programmed,' Dad explained, 'it can be locked in that mode until you decide to change it. There are 150 different modes' – Mum grinned as the dress flicked through them before their eyes – 'But with further development, it should be possible to have hundreds more!'

'I want one!' cried Elsie.

'It's incredible,' gasped Rorie.

The patterns stopped changing, but Mum remained fixed to the spot, grinning mischievously.

'Hey, don't stop,' pleaded Elsie. 'Do it again!'

But Mum just stood still, the dress fixed in the same

pattern.

'Oh, look!' said Rorie, just as Elsie was beginning to lose patience. 'Did you see that? The dress is—'

'Oh! It's getting longer!' cried Elsie.

Soon the hem of the dress reached almost to the floor. 'And...voila,' announced Mum. 'It's an evening dress!'

Elsie peered around the back for clues. 'How d'you *do* that?'

'You probably didn't notice,' explained Mum, 'but your Dad was sending the dress remote instructions from a device on his wrist. At the moment we can only make it long and short, but with further development you could program the same garment with dozens of different styles!'

'Hmm...the boots are all wrong,' Dad pointed out.

'Oh, of course!' said Mum, inspecting them. 'Silly me!' She clicked her heels together, like Dorothy in *The Wizard of Oz*. Immediately the long boots began to shorten, transforming into low-heeled shoes; next, the heels grew higher and narrower, until they were a perfect pair of evening shoes.

Elsie got down on her hands and knees. 'Wow! I want some o' them, too!'

'We call them "superbootshoes",' said Mum. She laughed. 'Oh, Arran, it works like a dream now!'

'Of course, there are all sorts of uses for this technology,' said Dad, removing his jacket. 'For instance, luggage can be reduced significantly.' He hung the jacket on a hook, then stood back and pointed the remote device at it. The jacket shivered slightly, then began to shrink. When it was child-sized, Dad took it off the hook and offered it to Elsie. 'Go ahead, try it on.'

'But how does it work?' asked Rorie.

'Organically,' said Dad. 'What makes a plant or animal remember the shape, colour and texture it is supposed to take – how, in other words, does a rose remember to become a rose, and not a cauliflower?'

'Pfff-ff-ff!' went Elsie. 'That's silly!'

'The answer, of course, lies in this...' said Dad, as a colourful twisted rope-ladder shape appeared on all three screens, rotating slowly. 'DNA, contained in every cell of every living thing, provides those instructions. But until now, it has not been possible to communicate those instructions to once-live cells – the wool that is no longer attached to a sheep, for example – or, indeed, to reverse or alter those instructions.'

'The suit is coded to grow and contract according to wireless instructions,' explained Mum. 'And the beauty of it is, it doesn't wear out. Because every time you switch, the cells renew themselves; dirt and sweat particles just get swallowed up, as the program knows they don't belong there.'

Elsie was admiring herself in the suit jacket. 'Hey, I wouldn't outgrow my clothes!'

'That's right,' said Mum. 'And no laundry – heaven! Do you realise what this means? With the right development, this could revolutionise the way we live.'

'This is just the start,' said Dad. 'Lols, you need to brief me again on that whole save-the-planet part of the presentation.'

'Sure,' agreed Mum, pulling off the superbootshoes. 'I'm pretty clear this week.'

Dad cleared his throat. 'No, I mean now.'

Mum looked up. 'Not now Arran; there's dinner, the dishes...got to put Elsie to bed...' she paused, noticing the sheepish look on Dad's face. 'What is it?'

'Well, you see I've, um...made us an appointment,' said Dad. 'With Rexco tomorrow, eleven o'clock.'

'No!' squealed Mum, making Rorie jump. 'You didn't...*seriously*?'

'I, er...yes. I had a hunch, you see...'

Mum's eyes were like saucers. 'How dare you!' she protested – but she was smiling.

'I didn't say anything, in case it all went wrong,' explained Dad. 'I didn't want to get your hopes up. Oh, and by the way girls,' he added, turning to them. 'You have to keep quiet about all this.'

'Keep quiet about it?!' exclaimed Rorie. 'You *are* joking, Dad? With blabber-mouth here?'

'I can too keep quiet about it!' insisted Elsie crossly.

Dad smiled. 'Come on Fluff; you wouldn't betray your old Dad now, would you?' Turning to Rorie, his expression was more solemn. 'Nobody must know about this until it's out there, you see; nobody. No matter what happens.'

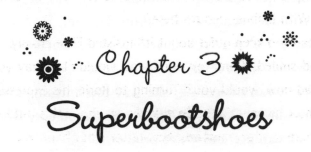

Chapter 3
Superbootshoes

The sign said:

TRAMLAWN SCHOOLS LTD
welcome you to
Poker Bute Hall

A security guard raised the barrier and they drove in.

In spite of everything, Elsie was swept along by the romantic majesty of the place; beautifully landscaped green lawns surrounded them on all sides, punctuated here and there by a lake, or a pavilion, or a magnificent old cedar tree. 'Wow! Is this all part of the school?'

Uncle Harris nodded. 'All 700 acres of it.'

As the grand old building itself appeared, Elsie gasped, 'You must be really rich!'

Aunt Irmine turned around, scowling. 'Don't be an idiot! It doesn't *belong* to us!'

Elsie turned scarlet. 'Oh.'

Rorie was furious, but forced herself to be polite. 'She *is* only seven years old, Aunt Irmine.'

'Well, for her information,' said Uncle Harris gruffly, 'we most certainly are *not* rich.'

Elsie wasn't listening; she was too entranced with the building. 'Ooh, it's like a palace, isn't it, Rorie? Hey, we can pretend we're princesses!'

Rorie grimaced. 'I want *my* school. I want Annie and Kristen and Lia.' She deeply resented the fact that she wouldn't even be able to contact any of her friends while at Poker Bute Hall; not only had her phone been confiscated, but Uncle Harris had explained that the school operated on a C.I.S. – a closed Internet system – which meant only Officially Approved Websites, and no outside chat. She felt as if she was on her way to a desert island.

Elsie shrugged. 'Well, *I'm* going to be a princess *anyway*, I am,' she declared, then told Uncle Harris, 'You can be king, if you like.'

Uncle Harris glared back at her through the rear-view mirror. 'What on earth are you on about?'

'Elsie was just imagining herself as the princess of the palace,' explained Rorie. 'The school, you see; it's very…palatial.'

'But it's *not* a palace,' scolded Aunt Irmine. 'It's a *school*.'

'Yes, I know, but—'

'A place for *learning*,' Aunt Irmine butted in. 'Pretending it's anything else is highly inappropriate.'

Rorie's mouth hung open. Was it really possible for someone to be so utterly cold and humourless?

'Wow, look at those chimblies!' cried Elsie, as they drew closer to the splendid Elizabethan building. 'I never seen chimblies like that before!'

'We'll have none of this silly baby talk,' snapped Uncle Harris. 'They're called *chimneys*.'

'Yeah!' nodded Elsie, gazing up at the tall multi-faceted red brick stacks. 'Chimblies!'

'Tut tut!' went Uncle Harris crossly as he parked the car.

Rorie felt a stab of sadness; how someone so lacking in fun and imagination as Uncle Harris could be Dad's brother, Rorie couldn't fathom. With Mum and Dad, this sort of childish mispronunciation was not only tolerated, it was positively celebrated. Everyone in their household ate platefuls of bisketti, or went to the hostipal, even though Elsie had outgrown these mistakes by now; they had become part of their private family language. Remembering this made

29

Rorie miss Mum and Dad so much, the pain in her chest all but took her breath away. And the agony of not knowing whether they were alive or dead...

Uncle Harris led them into a draughty, high-ceilinged room. With its stone pillars and enormous diamond-paned arched window, it reminded Rorie of a gothic church interior – only sparsely furnished with just ten rickety steel-framed beds and ten battered grey lockers. 'This is your dormitory, Aurora,' he said, addressing Rorie by her full name.

Rorie suddenly realised with alarm that she was going to have to share a room with nine other girls, none of which was Elsie. And what on earth was she going to do with Arthur Clarkson? Poor Arthur was still in her pocket, no doubt starving hungry...if she didn't get him out of there soon, he might have a complete nervous breakdown. Her only hope was that her roommates might like the idea of having a secret dorm pet, and not give the game away. Rorie bit her lip and prayed silently that they would.

'Well?' prompted Uncle Harris, irritably. 'Perhaps you might *share* your thoughts with us, Aurora?'

'Um...' *Think of something*...Rorie's eye was drawn to the stained glass coat of arms in the centre of the window, featuring a greyhound and a beetle, and the motto, *Una Via Rectus*. 'I was just wondering,' she said at last, 'what that motto on the window means?'

'Hmm, not well up on your Latin, I see,' scolded Uncle Harris, 'It's the school motto; it means "One Correct Way".'

'A fitting reminder,' added Aunt Irmine righteously, 'of this most important of all principles: that there is just one right way of doing things. That is what our pupils are here to learn.'

'That's not what Miss Frith said,' remarked Elsie. ''Cause when I was making my trannasaurus – we were doing dinosaurs last term – and I din't know what to use? She said there was *all sorts* of different ways I could choose...'

'Be quiet, Elsa,' said Uncle Harris.

'...Clay, cardboard, papier mache – or even—'

'QUIET!' bellowed Uncle Harris, silencing her instantly. 'I'm really not interested in the frivolous fripperies of your Miss Frith. There is a correct way and an incorrect way to do everything—'

'But—'

'...And before you ask, the correct way to *learn* about dinosaurs is to study the facts, not fiddle-faddling around with stupid amateur artwork. Complete waste of time! You don't learn to speak

31

French by building a model of the Eiffel Tower, now, do you?'

Rorie blinked at him, as she struggled to get her head around this argument. 'But...what about art...poetry? There's no one right way to paint a picture, or write a poem, is there?'

Uncle Harris waved his hand dismissively. 'No place for all that nonsense in the digital age. Why waste time painting a picture, when a camera or a computer can create anything you want? Or thinking up ever more preposterous ways of saying what's been said before anyway, when – even if such things were of any *use* – a computer program could do it for you in a fraction of the time? These things do not advance learning; school is not the place for them.'

'A place for everything, and everything in its place,' added Aunt Irmine, shaking her head.

Rorie exchanged a glance with Elsie; she wondered if she, too, was remembering Dad's words, when Rorie had asked him how he came up with his inventions. 'There are any number of ways to approach a problem,' he had said. 'You think long and hard enough about it, there's always an answer. Like, way back when people thought, wouldn't it be amazing to go to the moon? Well, they figured out a way to do it, didn't they?'

When Rorie had pointed out that there were lots of other people thinking long and hard about the same things as him, and not finding the answer, he'd shrugged. 'The way I work is different,' he began falteringly. 'I...get a *hunch* about something. Like a glimpse of a butterfly, and I have to follow it – I just *have* to, I'd go crazy if I didn't—'

'And some people think you're crazy if you *do*,' Mum had remarked.

Dad had nodded furiously. 'Oh yes. And sometimes you can't see the butterfly for a while, and you search and search. Then, *pop*! there it is again. And this time you're closer, and can see it more clearly...'

Nothing could be further from "One Correct Way", thought Rorie, picturing a butterfly.

Elsie had gazed into her father's eyes. 'Do people think *you're* crazy, Dad?'

'*Some* people...'

'That doesn't matter any more, Arran,' Mum had said softly.

'No...no.'

Once they were alone, Rorie let Arthur Clarkson out onto the small balcony outside the dorm window, and fed him some defrosted worms smuggled from home. She pulled a small branch from the nearby wistaria and put it down for him to climb on. The chameleon didn't move a muscle.

'Darker than ever,' Rorie remarked sadly.

'*Poor* Arfur,' said Elsie, trying to prod him into action with the wistaria.

'Leave him, Else,' said Rorie, stepping back inside. 'He needs time by himself.' She sighed and sat on the nearest bed, which creaked loudly as she did so. 'I can't believe Uncle Harris is our dad's brother,' she observed. 'It's like he's from another planet!'

'Planet Horrid,' said Elsie, stepping back through the window. 'Not Planet Wonderful, like, like…' She burst into tears and ran to Rorie. 'Oh, I want Daddy!' she wailed.

'Me too,' said Rorie, putting her arms around her little sister. She felt a sob swell up like a huge wave, breaking up her voice, but she took a deep breath and rode the crest of it as best she could. 'But Mum and Dad'll be back, I'm sure of it. Maybe there's been a mix-up at one of the hospitals, or something. It's *bound* to be something silly like that, Else; I just know it!' She would tell herself this over and over; she needed to believe it. Suddenly she felt overwhelmingly tired; it was now nearly twenty-four hours since they had returned from school to an empty house, and since then, one glimmer of hope after another had, in turn, been snuffed out, as they were informed by yet another hospital that no Arran and Laura Silk had been admitted there. She had not slept a wink.

She still could not quite believe that just forty-eight hours ago, the four of them had been together, full of anticipation for the big presentation...

Elsie prodded the button on the back of the cereal box, activating the video ad. *Hey, Nolita Newbuck here*, said the woman, accompanied by tinny music. *You can collect all eighteen of my superstar fashion cards...*

'Will you stop playing that thing!' complained Rorie.

'I like it,' insisted Elsie.

Mum stood at the kitchen mirror. 'Ugh...two hours' sleep; just look at the bags under my eyes!'

'Two hours!' exclaimed Rorie.

...Stars like Paloma Vega! India Hutton! said the cereal packet.

Rorie reached over and silenced it. 'Do *not* play it again,' she warned Elsie.

'There was so much work to do,' explained Mum. 'Oh, *my* hair...Arran, how dare you spring this on me; I'd have gone

35

to the hairdresser's!'

'I...er-herrm...' croaked Dad as he poured himself a third coffee. 'Oh no, tell me I'm not losing my voice! I cannot afford to lose my voice.'

'You're not losing your voice, Dad,' said Rorie, obligingly. 'You're just nervous, that's all.'

'Ooh, it's *sooo* exciting!' squealed Elsie. 'Can't I come with you, Mummy...Daddy? There's no important lessons in school today, honest!'

'Ha!' snorted Rorie.

Mum smiled wearily. 'Fluff, that would be lovely, but...good grief, is that the time?'

'Lols, we've got loads of time,' said Dad. 'It won't take us more than a couple of hours to get to Shenham, after we've dropped off the girls.'

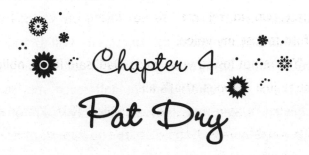

Chapter 4
Pat Dry

As usual on days when Mum was particularly busy, Rorie had collected Elsie from school. They turned up the garden path. 'Hey. Dad's car's not here.'

'Must be they din't get back yet,' remarked Elsie, with devastating powers of observation. 'Maybe they got stuck in traffic, or something.'

Rorie took out her phone and blinked at the empty screen. 'But they would have called me...look, nothing.' She let herself into the house. 'Maybe they've been back but popped out again for some reason...Mum?' she called into the eerily still, dark hallway. 'Dad?'

But the morning's dishes were still piled up in the kitchen sink. In the living room, the only sign of life was Arthur Clarkson's left eye as it swivelled in Rorie's direction. She put her hand on the home news sensor pad, and the screen lit up.

'Hello Rorie', it said, displaying its usual floating-colours pattern. 'There are two messages. Message one, received at eleven thirty-eight a.m.

[A man's face appeared] "Hi, this is Will Granger of Rexco for Arran Silk...Arran, just checking everything's OK; tried you on your Shel[1] and couldn't reach you, so just thought I'd try you here...anyway, possibly you're on your way..."'

Rorie felt her face flush the way it did when she was embarrassed – only this was a much weirder, darker feeling.

'Message two, received at 12.30 p.m.

[Will Granger's face appeared again, looking perplexed] "Hi, Arran...well, perhaps we got our lines twisted – or maybe something's come up and you've not been able to call me. Anyway, give me a call when you can, and we'll fix up another date. Bye now."'

Rorie's mouth went dry. Her mind ran through all the various possible explanations for where Mum and Dad might be, and why...nothing made sense.

But Elsie looked so forlorn, Rorie decided to put a brave face on it, for her sake. 'You're right', she said, as she began loading the dishwasher. 'They just got delayed. They were late getting to Rexco, so it follows that they're late getting back, that's all.' Any moment now, Mum and Dad would walk in, and everything would be all right. Meanwhile, she

---

[1] Stands for See Hear Everything Live. It's a phone, document file, camera, music and video player...a mini computer.

was *very* busy, and wouldn't even think about it.

Elsie sat staring out of the window.

Rorie handed her the Gem-Pops packet to put away. 'Come on, Else. A watched kettle never boils.'

'Do you take sugar, Inspector?' asked Maya, the neighbour, as the kettle came to a boil. Rorie had finally decided they needed to tell someone, and gone next door.

'Three, please,' said the policeman. 'I know; the wife's always giving me grief about it. Can't get enough of these, either,' he added, winking at Rorie as he pulled out a bag of butterscotch candy. 'Want one?'

'Thank you,' mumbled Rorie, not quite managing a smile as she reached into the bag. She was tied up in knots inside; she hoped the butterscotch would be soothing. Maya had been so kind when they had turned up on her doorstep, but Rorie could tell she was alarmed. Inspector Dixon, on the other hand, seemed perfectly relaxed as he took down the details. She found his air of quiet confidence at least somewhat reassuring.

'Right, well, I think I've got all the information I need for now,' said Dixon at last, consulting his smartpad. He smiled warmly at the girls. 'The main thing is, you're not to worry, OK?'

'OK,' muttered the girls, eyes downcast.

'Promise?' prompted Dixon, peering sideways at them.

'Promise.'

'Don't forget; the vast majority of people who disappear turn up within twenty-four hours.'

*Disappear, disappear...*The word went round and round in Rorie's head. *My parents have disappeared...*

'Meanwhile, we need to make some plans for you,' Inspector Dixon was saying.

'They can stay with us tonight, Inspector,' said Maya.

Dixon nodded. 'Excellent; thank you. I'll be back tomorrow – unless you hear something before then. There's bound to be a perfectly simple explanation for all this.'

A perfectly simple explanation.

How many times had Rorie heard that phrase over the past twenty-four hours? *Well, if there is one, no one's come up with it yet*, she thought. And now she was buried so far down that well of anxiety she thought she might suffocate.

'Well, I'm gonna find them!' declared Elsie. 'I'm not staying in this stinky place with stinky old Uncle Harris and stinky old Aunt Irmine!'

Rorie let Elsie cry a little, then said, 'And how are you going to do that? Don't you think this is the best place to be for now? Look, the police are searching for

Mum and Dad, and their pictures are already all over the newsnet. And you heard what Inspector Dixon said: sometimes people get amnesia; they forget who they are.'

Elsie frowned. 'But…couldn't they just look in their wallets to remind themselves?'

'Not if all their stuff got crushed in an accident.'

Elsie wiped her face with the back of her hand. 'Oh.' She thought some more. 'But…how can two people get amneezer at the same time?'

'Well, if they both got banged on the head…Inspector Dixon said he'd heard of it happening to people who have been in accidents.' Deep down, Rorie thought this would be a bit too much of a coincidence – she noticed that Dixon had only described it happening to *individuals* – but it was comforting to think it was possible, so she clung to the idea with every atom of her being.

There was a knock at the door. 'Uh…come in,' said Rorie.

A buxom blonde woman dressed in white appeared. 'Are you the Silk girls?' she asked.

'Yes.'

The woman's face crumpled, and she swished her way across to them, arms outstretched. 'Ohhh, you poor loves!' she cried. 'Mr Silk has just told me all about it...ohhh!' She took them by their heads and crushed them into her ample chest. She smelt of witch hazel mixed with a spicier, slightly nauseating smell. 'The agony...the agony!' she went on. 'Not knowing whether your parents are alive or dead! Not knowing if they've been smooshed to a pulp in a terrible crash! Mangled beyond recognition, their entrails spilling out all over the place...Ooohhh!'

This reminder of what might actually have happened to their parents brought fresh wails of agony from Elsie, and prompted Rorie to cry openly too.

'Never mind, never *mind*!' the woman went on, apparently believing she was a comfort to them. 'You'll be well looked after here, really you will...poor babies!' Releasing the girls and allowing them to breathe again, she took a wad of tissues from her pocket and began dabbing everyone's faces, including her own. 'I'm the nurse here,' she added, handing Rorie some more tissues. 'Pat dry.'

Rorie patted.

'No, I mean – well yes, go ahead, but, what I mean is, that's my name: Pat Dry. I'll see that you're all right, dears. And you must be Aurora?'

'It's Rorie, actually; only Uncle Harris and Aunt

Irmine call me Aurora, and I wish they wouldn't. But please – I know you mean to be kind, but could you just please not—'

'Oh, I squeezed you too hard, didn't I? I'm sorry, I can't help it; the girls here are so *starved* of affection—'

'No, what I mean is—'

'...Poor souls, such a deadly place! It's the only reason I stay, you know...*ghastly* school, can't imagine why anyone would want to send their child here...and you! With only an uncle like old Stick-Face for refuge now that you're probably orphans, and—'

'THAT!' said Rorie. 'C-could you just. Please. Not. Do that,' she said, shaking now – even, much to her own surprise, wagging a finger like an angry teacher. 'It...it isn't making it better, you know; all that talk of what might have happened to our parents.'

'And anyway it's not true,' added Elsie, blowing her nose loudly. 'They've got Amneezer, that's all.'

'Oh! Of course, how insensitive of me, I'm *so* sorry. Me and my big mouth, I always say too much. Luke – that's my son – he's always telling me off about it. "Mum," he says, "you're always opening your mouth and putting your foot in it." And he's right; he's right! I think that's why my Petesy left, because I couldn't open my mouth without...aargh!' Suddenly her eyes

43

were big and round. 'There's a...a creature out there!'

'The girls turned and looked. 'Oh don't worry about him,' said Elsie. 'That's just Arthur Clarkson.'

'*Arthur Clarkson*?!'

'Yes,' said Rorie. 'He's our pet chameleon...but *please* don't tell Uncle Harris about him; we're supposed to have returned him to the pet shop. I was hoping to find a more private spot for him – do you know of any?'

'Oh dear, this will never do, no no no!' tutted Pat as she bustled over to the window. 'I mean, if it were up to me, everyone could have a pet – we'd have a whole menagerie! But old Stick-Face – he'll never stand for it. Poor Arthur Clarkson'll be toast before you know it. And don't go thinking the other girls'll cover for you – they wouldn't dare!'

Rorie and Elsie gazed morosely at the chameleon; Rorie couldn't help forming a mental image of "Old Stick-Face" holding a long fork over a fire, with a blackened Arthur Clarkson on the end of it.

'I'll take him for you,' suggested Pat, picking him up. 'Luke can look after him, don't you worry; he works here, you know, he's the groundsman.'

'Well...all right,' said Rorie.

'Oh, *stinky* old Stick-Face!' declared Elsie angrily,

stamping her foot.

'Oh, there I go with my big mouth again,' said Pat. 'Don't ever let on I called him that, now will you?'

'Called him what?' came a familiar, sneering voice.

All three of them turned; there in the doorway, carrying some uniforms, was Uncle Harris.

Pat Dry quickly hid Arthur Clarkson behind her back, as if she were the naughty schoolgirl herself. 'Oh! Mr Silk, I didn't hear you come in...we were just talking about my Luke, and...I was telling the girls that, when they meet him, they mustn't let on that I called him...this funny thing, er...'

'Old Stick-Face?' said Uncle Harris stonily.

'Yes! That's it...because sometimes he does this thing where—'

'Nurse Dry,' interrupted Uncle Harris, putting the uniforms down and stepping forward. 'What are you hiding behind your back?'

Rorie exchanged a guilty glance with Elsie.

'My...my hands!' said Pat, stepping backwards. 'They're just a bit grubby, that's all – I didn't want you to see them, I'm ever so sorry. I'll go and wash them right away, sir.' She edged towards the door.

'*How* dirty?' asked Uncle Harris, barring her way. 'Show me!'

Rorie could stand it no longer. 'It's Arthur Clarkson,' she blurted out. 'We lied to you, Uncle, I'm sorry. We didn't want to get rid of him, you see.'

Sheepishly, Pat Dry brought the chameleon forward for him to see.

Uncle Harris's face went a mottled purple; he turned his flaming eyes to Rorie and Elsie. 'You lied! How dare you!'

'Oh now, Mister Silk—' pleaded Pat.

'I will not tolerate insubordination!' snapped Uncle Harris. 'That includes you, Nurse Dry!'

Pat was defiant. 'I was only going to give him to Luke to look after.'

'No!' barked Uncle Harris.

'Oh, horrid Stick-Face!' cried Elsie, bursting into tears. 'You're not my uncle, I hate you! I want my Mum and Da-ha-had!'

Pat rushed over to comfort her, and turned to Uncle Harris angrily. 'Oh, you see what you've done? Don't you think these poor girls are in enough distress already, without adding to it like this?'

'If they have not been brought up to show respect where it's due, then it's about time they learned!' said Uncle Harris. Then, to the girls: 'At least *I* have a sense of honour and duty, which is why you two are here.

The lizard must go!'

He reached for the chameleon.

But Arthur Clarkson wasn't having any of it: to the girl's amazement, he suddenly turned a violent red colour and appeared to double in size as he raised himself up on his surprisingly long stick-like legs. The crest on his neck stood on end, and he opened his wide mouth and hissed so loudly, Uncle Harris lurched back, his face stricken with horror.

'Aaagh!' he cried, then attempted to compose himself. 'Yes well, you can get rid of it, nurse. *Ahem.* But if I find that thing *anywhere* in the school grounds,' he bellowed, 'you'll be out of a job, do you hear!'

Chapter 5
Not Very Uniform

'Hi, I've been asked to come and get you,' said the girl. She was the first pupil Rorie and Elsie had seen, since they had arrived during lesson time, and Uncle Harris hadn't bothered to show them round the school. She was about Rorie's age, and wore what looked like a very old-fashioned games kit; a polo shirt and green skirt with straps going over the shoulders. Tall with short dark hair, she might have been pretty but for the snootily upturned nose and sneer on her lips. 'Oh, I see you're not ready yet,' she remarked abruptly, clearly disinterested in exchanging any pleasantries.

'Ready?' echoed Rorie.

'Yah. For dinner,' replied the girl, with a detached air of superiority.

'Oh, OK,' said Rorie, stepping forward. 'We're ready.'

48

'Ahem.' The girl sidestepped, blocking Rorie's way.

Rorie tried to go round her, but the girl blocked her again. 'Ha ha!' responded Rorie, uncertainly.

But the girl just sighed irritably, pointing to the uniforms that lay on the bed. 'You're supposed to be in uniform. I don't have time to wait; you'll have to make your own way there. Down the stairs, go to the end of the corridor, up one flight, then down the galleria to the Tzikan Wing, past the library and down again, through the double doors and the refectory's at the other end of the quad. Bye.'

She was gone before Rorie and Elsie had a chance to take all this in.

'What's a quad?' asked Elsie.

Rorie sighed. 'I don't know; I think it's a kind of four-wheeled bike. Come on, let's get changed; I'm actually feeling hungry now.' Only now did she realise she had barely eaten anything for over twenty-four hours.

They were late for dinner, having got hopelessly lost trying to follow the snooty girl's instructions. And when they arrived, everybody stared. Stifled giggles echoed around the beige walls.

Rorie looked at the other girls' uniforms, then at

her own and Elsie's; they had everything on the wrong way. Her skin tingled with embarrassment. Nothing had been familiar, and since the one girl they'd met had been in a different outfit, they had no clues.

There had been a stiff starchy shirt with twelve fiddly buttons (they had never dealt with buttons before) and an even stiffer, starchier collar the size of a nun's wimple. Did this go *under* the skirt-with-bib-thing, or *over it*? And did you wear the 'bib' part at the back or the front? There were tights; awful white things which hung in dewlaps around Elsie's skimpy little legs. Tights! *Nobody* wore tights any more, not since the invention of spray-ons. Then there were two mysterious strips of fabric: one wide, black silk one, and one thinner, green one. Rorie supposed the latter to be a tie, as worn in old movies, though she hadn't a clue how to do it up; she just did a double knot. Elsie decided that since all the people wearing ties in old movies were men, *she* would tie her hair in bunches with the two odd strips of fabric.

'That looks weird,' Rorie remarked.

'I don't care,' shrugged Elsie. 'I'm gonna start a fashion.'

Rorie felt a twinge of admiration. Part of her wished she could be a little more like her little sister, so confident in her individuality, not caring what others thought of her. Rorie cared deeply about fitting in; to stand out in any way was mortifying for her. Fate had dealt her a particularly mischievous hand, however, because she *did* stand out; she couldn't help it. She had the kind of face that was quite improbable in its loveliness; not what you would call perfect, because 'perfect' suggests a humdrum orderliness of features, and Rorie's face was anything but humdrum or orderly. It was more like a starkly original design, with unusually high, sweeping brows and pale, almond-shaped eyes. A conventional mouth wouldn't fill so much of a face, nor would it have a gap between the front teeth, yet these imperfections only made her more striking.

It was as if all the beauty genes had been doled out in one great lump, and there were none left over for Elsie. Instead of full, red lips, Elsie had thin, pale ones. Instead of an elegant, aquiline nose, Elsie had a blobby-looking thing. Her skin tended to be dry, pale and flaky, and her hair – unlike Rorie's luxuriant chestnut-brown locks – was a scarecrow's thatch.

Yet Elsie knew how to divert people's attention away from her gorgeous big sister; she'd had seven years' practice at it. What was more, she was apparently the one who had inherited every last drop of their parents' creativity. If Rorie had been asked to paint a tree at the age of seven, she would have made a brown trunk topped by a green blob. Not Elsie; her trees were incredible fantasy things with snaking branches writhing this way and that, all bursting with carefully drawn leaves and fruits, different every time. Rorie might have possessed beauty, but Elsie knew how to create it.

So there they stood, with almost everything on back-to-front or in the wrong place, in front of a whole school full of people who believed that there was One Correct Way of doing things. Rorie felt her face burn furiously.

'You're *late*,' sneered Uncle Harris.

'It's not our fault!' squealed Elsie. 'First we couldn't find the Chicken Wing or the four-wheeled bike, then we didn't know where the factory was!'

Her mistakes prompted loud snorts of derision from the Poker Bute Hall girls. Rorie wanted the ground to swallow her up.

'Never you mind, dears,' said Pat Dry, bustling over. 'We'll find something for you to eat.'

Uncle Harris rolled his eyes. 'Tuh! Well, I suggest they adjust their attire appropriately first, Nurse.'

Having had a few leftover morsels scraped together for her, Rorie approached a table, where she noticed a girl who sat apart from everyone else, reading. She wore her black hair in lots of little braids and decorated with assorted charms. Rorie was instantly drawn to her, not just because of her unusual appearance, but because, right now, she seemed as much of an outsider as Rorie herself. But as soon as she sat down, another girl rushed up to her. 'Hi, I'm Alison Clinghorn. Can I sit next to you?'

Since Alison Clinghorn had already taken her plate and gone half the length of the refectory table to get there, and since there was a free seat, Rorie shrugged and said, 'OK.'

The girl with the braids pocketed her ebook, smiled an inner smile, and left.

Disappointed, Rorie turned to Alison and introduced herself. 'We're just here temporarily, me and my sister...'

'Oh, I remember *my* first day,' Alison gushed, not hearing. 'I was *sooo* nervous...and I couldn't tie my cravat right' – she tugged at the black silk – 'Oooh, I could've died! But you'll soon get used to it. It's horrible being new, isn't it?'

'There are worse things,' said Rorie, a wave of pain

assaulting her as she thought afresh of her parents. Pain and panic; helpless, desperate longing. But she felt grateful that at least someone in the room wasn't looking down on her. 'Have you been here long?'

'This is my second year,' said Alison. 'It's strict, but you get used to it. You're on this table, so that means we're in the same class and the same dorm. I'll help you; I'll ask if we can sit next to each other. Won't that be fun?'

'Oh...thanks,' said Rorie.

There was a ripple of applause from the other side of the refectory. Rorie and Alison both looked up to see what was going on, and saw that a tall blonde girl had just entered the room. She acknowledged her reception with the slight, relaxed smile of one very used to such admiration – the opposite of the big, gauche beam that now spread across Alison Clinghorn's face as she clapped along with the rest of them. 'Oh, it's Nikki Deeds!' she gushed. 'She just got back from the regional athletic awards; that's why she's late. She won the gold medal in the triathlon for the *third time*. She's amazing!'

Rorie applauded politely. She watched as Nikki Deeds drew nearer, occasionally stopping to exchange pleasantries along the way. She looked a few years older than Rorie, and was wearing the same games kit as the girl they'd met earlier. Elegant and finely chiselled, Nikki Deeds had tightly-wound white-blonde hair and freckled, flushed cheeks. As she wafted by, Rorie noticed that a badge on her shirt said 'PERFECT'.

'"Perfect?"' quoted Rorie, perplexed.

'Yes,' said Alison Clinghorn. 'There are only six Perfects in the whole school; it's really hard to become one. I want to be one some day!'

Rorie shook her head slowly. 'This place really is very different from my usual school.'

'It's different from most schools,' said Alison, solemnly. 'The standards are incredibly high; I've learned *so much*. Hey, maybe your parents will really like it, and decide to let you stay!'

'I...doubt it,' said Rorie. Skipping the subject of what might or might not have happened to her parents, she went on; 'For one thing, it seems they don't believe in any sort of creative work here.'

'Good thing too!' said Alison cheerfully. 'All that sort of thing is *play*, not work – it took me a while to understand that, but now I couldn't imagine things any other way. What's your favourite subject, then? Mine's Systems,' Alison prattled on, not waiting for an answer. 'I just love cataloguing! When I graduate I want to be a systems librarian...it's so fascinating!'

Rorie paused mid-munch. 'Er...what are the *un-*exciting lessons like?'

Alison didn't get what Rorie was driving at. 'Oh, not bad really...the thing I thought I'd *never* get used to is the cold showers or the housework drill at five-thirty a.m., but you do! I'm the fastest floor polisher in the class; I won a prize for it. I bet you'd be good at it too; hey! We can have a race, you and me!' She linked arms with Rorie and did a sort of scrunched-up-grin-and-shoulder-hunch that seemed to say, 'We're going to be the best of pals, I just *know* it!'

Three tables away, Elsie was having a hard time fitting in.

'My dad's an inventor,' she announced to anyone who cared to listen. 'And my mum too.'

The other girls looked at her the way cows observe passing hikers; quietly detached, munching, mildly curious.

'They've gone away on a secret mission that's top secret and highly confident,' Elsie continued. 'So me and Rorie, we're only going to be here a little while, till the mission's over.'

'What sort of inventors?' asked one girl.

'Well, I'm not allowed to say, but they invent magic cloves. Things that make you disappear and stuff, and that's why they're needed for spies.' She thought for a moment, not quite satisfied with this, then added, 'They *might* have to do some spying theirselves.'

The table fell silent for a moment. Then another girl said, 'If you're not allowed to say, then why did you just tell us that?'

Elsie summoned the best response she could think of. 'No, I mean it's OK for me to say about some things, but not others. There's other things I *could* say about, but I'm not, see.'

Silence again. 'What, other things more secret than spying?' asked the girl, perplexed.

Elsie sighed, and looked around the table. She'd never known such a bad audience. Usually stories like these would have a group huddled excitedly around her, hanging on her every word. Not coldly testing her like this. What *was* the matter with these people? She would just have to divert the whole conversation. 'Once?' she began, 'My mum, right, she had to go on a mission, and she had these boots that were *killer* boots, right, and there was *snake poison* in the toe so all she had to do was kick somebody and they fell

57

down dead. And once?' Elsie lowered her voice in hushed reverence. 'She actually *killed* somebody.'

The whole table gasped with genuine horror – not the mock horror barely concealing delight such stories would usually generate. Then something happened that Elsie had never experienced in her entire life; everyone went back to eating and talking among themselves, and completely ignored her.

Chapter 6
Moll

After dinner, the girls were called into Uncle Harris's office. Rorie felt her heart jump like a rabbit: Inspector Dixon was with him.

Elsie rushed up to him. 'Have you found our mum 'n' dad?'

Dixon patted her on the head and smiled sadly. 'No Elsie, I'm sorry, we haven't.'

Uncle Harris, who was adjusting a display of what looked like instruments of torture on his wall, seemed sorry too – though not, Rorie reckoned, for the right reasons.

'Come! Sit with me,' said Dixon, indicating the couch; the girls sat. 'I just wanted to reassure you that we are doing everything possible to find out what has happened to your parents,' he said in his soothing, gentle voice. 'Meanwhile, I'm sure you're being well looked after here.'

Rorie and Elsie looked at each other doubtfully, but Uncle Harris narrowed his eyes at them while polishing one of the torture devices. It gleamed at them menacingly.

'Now, as you know, there were no serious road accidents reported on Monday morning, either in the vicinity of your home or that of Rexco.' Inspector Dixon went on, oblivious as he consulted his smartpad. 'Although we have no way of knowing exactly what route your parents took along the approximately eighty kilometres between the two, our team have been scrutinising the two or three routes they were most likely to have taken. Although two accidents did take place, neither was serious, and neither one involved your father's car.'

Rorie gasped with relief.

'So they're OK then?' trilled Elsie, wide-eyed with excitement.

Inspector Dixon stirred some sugar into his tea. 'Well...I wouldn't go jumping to any conclusions, Elsie,' he said gently. 'They haven't actually, *ahem*...turned up yet.'

'Oh.' Elsie stared at the floor.

There was a moment's silence, then the Inspector

said, 'We can, however, make other checks to determine what we can about the route they took. And the more accurate the information we have regarding timing, the better. Now, you say your parents dropped you off at Elsie's school at 8:45, is that correct?'

'Yes,' said Rorie confidently. 'I know because I checked just as we were getting out of the car. I remember having exactly five minutes to get to my school after Elsie went in with her friends.'

'And you say your parents were going straight from the school to Rexco?' asked Dixon. 'Is it possible they went home first?'

Rorie and Elsie looked at each other; Elsie shrugged. 'I don't think so,' said Rorie. 'I mean, they weren't headed in that direction.'

'...But it's *possible* that they may have forgotten something and turned back?' prompted Dixon.

The possibility hadn't occurred to Rorie until now. She pictured Dad, so groggy from lack of sleep; Mum all flustered. *Now, where did I put those superbootshoes?* 'Well, they might have, I suppose—'

Inspector Dixon's Shel beeped; he answered it. 'Hi Greg...Yes, I'm with them now...'

Rorie felt her skin prickle all over.

'Really?' said Dixon. 'What time? And the

location? Mmm-hmm…yes, do pass it on. Excellent, well done…all right, speak to you later.' He turned to the girls. 'Well, it seems at last we have something to go on. Your father's car was caught by a speed camera on a road about six kilometres south of the Rexco headquarters.'

The girls gasped.

Dixon consulted his Shel. 'And…there it is.' He showed them the image that had just uploaded onto the screen. It was unmistakable: Dad's car.

'160!' exclaimed Uncle Harris, noting the recorded speed. 'Well well…'

'In a ninety-kilometre-an-hour zone,' added Dixon. 'Seems they were running late, too, judging by the time.'

'Tut-tut-tut, that's typical of Arran, that is. Typical! Never had any sense of time!'

'Oohhh!' wailed Elsie, bursting into tears.

Rorie put her arm around her. 'But Dad wouldn't—'

'Tuh! You don't know the half of it,' Uncle Harris sneered. 'He's always charged around like a bloomin' lunatic; clearly didn't learn his lesson!'

'Mister Silk!' retorted Inspector Dixon. 'May I ask that you *please* consider your nieces' feelings!' He turned to the girls. 'As I have said: we know there weren't any serious accidents reported in the area,' he said soothingly, offering them butterscotch. 'Don't forget that.'

The common room was another grand, high-ceilinged room, not much cosier than the dorm. It was the last place Rorie wanted to be right now; she wanted to have her own quiet bedroom to retreat to, so she could think about everything. *Perhaps everyone will leave me alone anyway*, she told herself. Although she was still curious about the girl with the braids; she wouldn't mind talking to her. But she could see no sign of her. Alison didn't seem to be around either – which was actually something of a relief. Other girls were either studying or playing virtual chess; one sat on the floor doing some elaborate stretches, while three others were chatting together. Rorie found herself a quiet window seat and sat down, hoping to be ignored, but after a moment the three girls came over.

'Hi, I'm Caroline,' said one girl.

'And I'm Caroline,' said another.

'And I'm Caroline,' said the third. Then the three of them looked at each other and tittered like birds.

Rorie groaned inwardly. 'Oh-kay, so you're all called Caroline. Are you really, or is it a joke?'

'No: we *really are*!' snorted Caroline number one. Once again, the three of them creased up.

'Amazing,' said Rorie flatly; clearly there wasn't much in the way of laughs to be had around here. 'My name's Rorie.'

'Really?' said Caroline number two. 'I thought that was a…a *boy's name*!' The sheer hilarity of a girl with a boy's name sent her into paroxysms; the others followed suit.

Rorie could contain her irritation no longer. 'You don't get out much, you lot, do you?'

Caroline number two blinked at her. 'I'm sorry?'

Stupid girl! Rorie told herself. Did she want to make friends here, or not? Not particularly; she wanted her *real* friends. But since there was no possibility of contact with them, these people would have to do instead. She would have to try harder. She forced a smile. 'That is, I, uh…my name is actually short for Aurora. It means Dawn; I thought about changing my name to Dawn, so I wouldn't always have to explain to people, you know, "yeah, I know it's really a boy's name, *but…*"' Aware she was now trying too hard, she nevertheless went on, 'but I didn't really *feel* like a Dawn, so I just stuck with Rorie—'

'Actually, we do get out – *a lot*,' said a stony voice

behind her. Rorie turned round to see a tall girl with short black hair; the one who was doing the fancy stretches before. She bristled, recognising her as the one who had been sent to fetch her and Elsie for dinner earlier. The girl put out a hand. 'I'm Joyce,' she said. 'So. You're Mr Silk's niece?'

'Oh, uh...yes,' replied Rorie falteringly. She suddenly realised with alarm that she had no idea what, if anything, the Poker Bute Hall girls knew about her circumstances. Knowing she couldn't possibly share her grief and anxiety over her parents' disappearance with a bunch of complete strangers – especially such weird ones – she added, 'My sister and I are just staying here for a sort of...cultural exchange thing. For a while.'

'Cultural exchange?' said Joyce. 'That's odd.' She turned to the Carolines. 'No one from here has gone away, have they?'

The Carolines all shrugged and shook their heads.

'Well, it's just a sort of...trial thing,' Rorie explained. 'My dad and Uncle...Mr Silk, thought it might be interesting for us to, you know, see what it's like.'

Joyce just stood, arms folded, staring at Rorie. 'Really?' There was an awkward silence. 'Well, there's a few things you clearly haven't found out yet. Ever played Hammerball?' she asked.

'Hammerball?'

'They don't play it at your school?' asked Caroline number three, incredulously.

'No.'

'There's a lesson first thing tomorrow,' said Joyce. 'We also do athletics, archery, martial arts...oh, we get out *a lot*.'

Hostile – and dumb, too – thought Rorie. She didn't even understand what she'd meant by 'getting out'.

Joyce took a step closer. 'You know, just because you're the head teacher's niece, you needn't think you're superior, because frankly you're a know-nothing around here. You know Nikki Deeds – the Perfect?'

'I, uh, know *of* her.'

'Yeah right. Well, *I* happen to know her really well. Nikki and I are good friends; we tell each other everything.'

Oh-kay! Thanks for the tip! thought Rorie, as Joyce turned and walked away. Just about the only thing that was missing from this petty little piece of one-upmanship was a big raspberry.

The mood was swiftly changed when Alison

appeared. 'Hi Rorie!' she trilled, rushing over and hooking her arm through Rorie's. The Carolines lost interest and resumed their twittering among themselves. 'I was looking for you!' gushed Alison. 'I thought maybe you'd got lost again.'

'Well I did, a bit,' admitted Rorie; she had been trying to find Pat Dry, so she could ask how Arthur Clarkson was getting on, but had to give up in the end. 'Um, Alison...what's Hammerball?'

'Oh, we've got that tomorrow, haven't we? Whoa, straight in at the deep end, eh?' she laughed. 'Well, it's rough, but you get used to it...'

Rorie wished Alison wouldn't keep insisting she would get used to this or that aspect of Poker Bute Hall life; in the first place, she hated to think of the possibility she'd be staying long enough to get used to it, and secondly, she was convinced this was a place she could *never* get used to anyway.

'Well, I'd love to tell you all about it,' said Alison, gathering up her things. 'But I'm late for cataloguing masterclass. Byeee!'

Rorie watched her leave, then turned and was confronted with the mysterious girl with the jet-black braids. 'Oh! I didn't see you.'

'Sorry, didn't mean to pounce!' said the girl,

stepping back slightly. She had a slender, wispy frame; although she was in school uniform, she somehow made it look stylish, almost as if she'd chosen the outfit herself. Rorie couldn't quite figure out how this was, but the overall "Dracula's little sister" effect was intriguing. 'Guess I kind of blend in when I'm mooching about down there,' the girl added. She waved her hand in the direction of a secluded little nook in the back. 'Here,' she said, handing Rorie an ebook. 'Thought you'd want to take a look at this.'

Rorie read the title: *Hammerball: the Rules*. 'Hey, thanks, uh…?'

'Moll,' said the girl. She leaned closer. 'Steer clear of *that* one, if you can,' she whispered, jerking her head toward Joyce. 'She's a Rottweiler.'

Rorie winced. 'Oh; I think I'm already on her bad side.'

Moll grimaced sympathetically. 'Noticed that.'

Rorie fidgeted with the ebook. 'I'm Rorie.'

'Yeah, I know,' said Moll. 'Heard you talking to Alison Clingfilm.'

Rorie couldn't help laughing at the nickname. 'Oh, but she *means* well…I think.'

Moll rolled her eyes. 'Drives me *nuts*.' She slumped down into the nearest easy chair. 'But then, this whole place does.'

At last! thought Rorie. Here was someone she could relate to. She fell to her knees and huddled up to the armrest. 'Me too!' she cried. 'I mean, what *is* it with these people?'

'It's supposed to be this "Big Breakthrough" in education. "The Way of the Future".' Moll rolled her eyes. 'And people like my foster parents buy into it, big time. Pah! Well *I* don't buy it. I think there's something much more...' Moll trailed off, regarding Rorie with caution; Rorie could sense her backing down. 'Ah, what do I know?' said Moll at last. 'Look, best thing is just to try and fit in. Don't be like me; I'm a disaster!'

'But why is everyone so—'

'Well well, what do we have here?' came a voice from behind her. Rorie looked up; it was Joyce. 'The weirdo club! Look everybody! Moll's made a new friend. Isn't that nice?'

Moll's face hardened; she stood up and moved away. 'Catch you later,' she said, tapping Rorie on the shoulder.

Rorie saw a deep sadness in her big brown eyes.

Chapter 7
The Golden Girl

Elsie was never very interested in puzzles, and that seemed to be all there was to do in her common room; either that or reading, and she wasn't big on that, either. All the other girls were engrossed in one or other of these activities when she walked in. What Elsie badly wanted was to play dress-up; her way of coping with unpleasant realities was simply to invent more appealing ones for herself, and dress-up was the best way to do that. Otherwise, every moment would be filled with the pain of worrying over her parents, and that made her feel sick. It also made her want to cry, and she was determined not to do that in front of these stuck-up Poker Bute Hall girls.

''Scuse me,' she asked one of them. 'Where's the dress-up stuff?'

'The what?'

'Dress-up stuff,' said Elsie. 'You know, princess dresses, fairy cloves…'

The girl shrugged. 'Haven't seen any.' She went back to arranging the pieces of her 3D virtual puzzle.

Elsie then approached an older girl who sat at a computer in the middle of the room. Her face resembled a boiled potato, save for a pair of wire spectacles, and she wore her brown hair in a short, severe bob. She wore a badge which said 'PERFECT'. ''Scuse me,' asked Elsie, 'but can you tell me where's the dress-up stuff?'

The Perfect gave her a withering look. 'Oh, you're the new girl; Elsa, isn't it?'

'Elsie.'

'I'm Leesa Simms, your Perfect supervisor. There are plenty of *intelligent* games for you to play with here, but nothing pointless or frivolous such as you're suggesting. Besides, Poker Bute Hall girls are required to wear uniform at all times.'

Elsie was aghast. 'What, even in bed?'

'Don't be insolent!' snapped Leesa Simms.

Several girls sniggered; Elsie stuck out her tongue at them.

Leesa Simms punched some keys on the computer. 'One demerit, Elsa Silk; I saw that. Two more, and you

71

get a detention.'

At that moment, Uncle Harris walked in. 'Well, well, what's going on here?'

Both Elsie and Leesa Simms began to speak at the same time, but they were silenced when Uncle Harris did something truly shocking: he *smiled*.

'Oh well, never mind,' he said, suddenly all cuddly and genial. 'Elsa, could I have a private word, please?'

Elsie blinked at him, unable to reconcile this Uncle Harris with the one she had been with in his office only a few minutes ago. Then she noticed that Rorie was with him. 'Oh, um...OK.' She got up and trotted hurriedly over to them.

'Now then, girls,' said Uncle Harris as he closed the door, his face still creased into the strange contortion of a smile that looked about as much at home on his face as a duck in a desert. 'Your Aunt Irmine and I feel we, ah, may have got off on the wrong footing with you...and I know you've not had much to eat. Why don't you both come and have some tea and cake with us?'

'No tha—' began Elsie, but Rorie clamped a hand over her mouth.

'Thank you,' said Rorie. 'We'd love to.'

'Ahem. I realise this has been a tough time for you two,' said Uncle Harris, passing the cake.

'It's not easy for any of us,' added Aunt Irmine, with that head-shake of hers.

What a nerve! thought Rorie. How dare she try to suggest there was any comparison between what Rorie and Elsie were going through, and her own situation! *Horrible old bat.*

'I want to go home,' said Elsie, pouting.

'Now, Elsa, you know we can't let you go home,' said Uncle Harris with exaggerated patience. 'You can't live there alone; it's against the law.'

'Want to go home.' It was as if Elsie hadn't heard.

'...But Irmine and I *have* decided to give you the morning off tomorrow,' added Uncle Harris.

'Hey! We can visit our home, then!' said Elsie, perking up.

'I don't want to do that,' said Rorie quickly. 'I'd find it upsetting.' To *go* there was one thing – but to have to leave again would be unbearable. Her eye was drawn to a display case of butterflies on the wall. Beautiful butterflies. Dead ones.

'I'm afraid we can't go anyway, even for the morning,' said Uncle Harris. 'The fact is, we have a different trip organised.'

Rorie turned back. 'We do?'

'Yes. *Ahem*, actually, we're going to pay a visit to my grandmother...your great-grandmother.'

Rorie almost choked on her cake.

'We can't visit her,' said Elsie, who was too young to have known her great-grandmother before she'd gone into a nursing home. 'It's not allowed.'

Uncle Harris looked surprised. 'Not allowed?'

'Um, what Elsie means,' said Rorie, 'is that Dad doesn't...didn't...doesn't bring us when he goes.'

'He says she's Too Far Gone,' added Elsie.

Uncle Harris and Aunt Irmine exchanged glances. 'Well!' said Aunt Irmine sniffily. 'I shan't say what I think about that.'

The implication of this was only too clear to Rorie, and the anger bubbled up again. 'Are you suggesting—'

'Now, now, we're not suggesting there's anything wrong with your father not bringing you to the nursing home,' said Uncle Harris hastily, with another one of those strange smiles. 'Just that...he and I do things differently, that's all. Well, it's all arranged; we leave after breakfast.'

Clangalangalanggg!!! All around Rorie went the ringing noise, jangling her bones. She sat bolt upright and screamed into the darkness. Where was she? Was there a fire?

Then her eyes adjusted and she realised she was in her dorm at Poker Bute Hall, and nobody else seemed in the least bit alarmed; some of them were snickering. Rorie felt embarrassment, followed quickly by a heavy, sinking feeling; sheer dread over what the day would bring. She shivered: the room was icy, and her toes were numb.

The lights came on and there, beaming at her from the next bed, was Alison. 'Hey, nothing to be scared of!' she said, pulling herself up. 'It's just the wake-up bell.'

'What time is it?' asked Rorie.

'Five-thirty,' said Alison. 'We have to fit in housework drill before breakfast – remember?' She rolled her eyes in a good-humoured way; whatever the absurdities of Poker Bute Hall life, she seemed to take such enormous pride in being a part of it that she would put up with anything.

Five-thirty! It felt like the middle of the night – no, it *was* the middle of the night, as far as Rorie was concerned. 'Oh, I don't have to get up,' she said, flopping back down onto the cardboardy pillow. 'I've got the morning off.'

Alison yanked her back up cheerfully. 'Uh-uh!' she sang. 'It says on the register you've got morning *lessons* off…that's not till after breakfast!'

Rorie groaned. She had assumed that Uncle Harris had meant the *whole* morning; apparently not. 'Don't they have robots?' she asked blearily.

'No; the robots monitor us while *we* do the job instead,' explained Alison. 'It's all part of our fitness regime. Poker Bute Hall is the top school in the country for physical fitness, did you know that? Plus, it's good discipline…hurry up, we mustn't be late for drill call! It's OK,' she added jovially. 'You get—'

'Used to it,' said Rorie heavily. 'Uh-huh.'

It was the tallest ladder Rorie had ever had to climb, and she was terrified. She forced herself to concentrate on the window she was leaning against, and not the floor that was so far beneath her – or else she just knew she would faint. Staring at her hand as it clutched the cloth, she tried to send it a message to move, but it stubbornly refused.

The supervising robot was fast approaching, barking out its orders in Aunt Irmine's voice, '*Get on with it! No malingering!*' No doubt the real Aunt Irmine was still blissfully asleep in her bed. Rorie felt a jolt, as the robot rattled her ladder. '*Come along, no sleeping on the job!*' it nagged. Rorie swayed alarmingly, but at least it got her arm moving, and once started she couldn't stop. *How crazy is this place?* she thought as she rubbed furiously, now a boiling stew of anger, fear and anxiety. Did her aunt and uncle have no compassion?

It was at that moment that Rorie, from her vantage point overlooking the athletics field, caught sight of the golden girl.

She was alone, practising the high jump; Rorie soon recognised her as Nikki Deeds, champion athlete of Poker Bute Hall. Rorie was captivated by her moves as she thrust down the support, twisted skyward – amazingly high! – then soared over the pole in a perfect, elegant arc. It was almost as if she were flying; dancing on air like a goddess. Rorie knew nothing about this girl's life, yet found it impossible to imagine that anything ever went wrong for her. She seemed so secure, so in control. Life was wonderful, and here she was, happily throwing herself into the air with abandon.

With a sharp stab, Rorie realised how desperately she longed to trade places with her.

Chapter 8
Philip, Tony and the Corgis

'Oh, what a pretty girl,' said Great-Grandma, clasping Rorie's hand in her dry, leathery hand with its rigid, unyielding fingers. 'Who did you say she was again?'

'She's Arran's daughter, Grandma,' said Uncle Harris loudly. 'Auro...Rorie.'

Rorie felt the old lady's hand tremble in her own; a rhythmic wobble, almost as if she were constantly turning an invisible handle. Great-Grandma was 112 years old.

The old lady's face lit up. 'Ah, yes, of course!' Seconds later, confusion clouded her face once more. 'Who's Arran?'

'He's my brother, Grandma...your grandson,' replied Uncle Harris, the fixed grin on his face slowly turning sour.

'Ah!' said Great-Grandma, satisfied at last.

Elsie shifted in her seat, making a squeaky noise. Rorie hoped this wouldn't take very long, or Elsie might cause mischief, crash into some zimmer-framed old dear or something. Rorie could tell she was finding this all just as uncomfortable as she was herself. The place had an unpleasant odour; yeasty, steamy kitchen smells mingling with antiseptic and stale flowers, all masking something much more unsavoury. And it was stiflingly hot; Uncle Harris opened a window.

Great-Grandma was from that era when wealthy ladies still got their faces surgically stretched, but never managed to do anything about seemingly less important parts of their bodies, like their necks and their hands. So while her face had a rather goldfish-like appearance – albeit sagging now – her neck was a mass of folds and wrinkles, and the gnarled blue veins stood out from the backs of her hands like trapped worms. Her transparent pink hair was teased into the standard old-lady style – short and spiky with gel – and over a loose pair of black trousers she wore a very old, richly patterned silk kimono that, like Great-Grandma herself, might have been beautiful once. On the table in front of her were assorted packages of fancy soaps and chocolates; Uncle Harris had been generous with his gifts.

'Yes, very pretty!' remarked Great-Grandma again, admiring Rorie. 'Not like that one over there,' she added, waggling a wobbly finger in Elsie's direction. 'Poor dear,' she added in a conspiratorial tone, 'she is so very plain, isn't she?'

'Oh, she isn't, Great-Grandma,' said Rorie hastily. 'Perhaps your eyesight is failing you. Elsie's lovely!'

The old lady peered.

'She's also very talented,' added Rorie, sensing that Great-Grandma was about to come out with another put-down. '*Amazingly* talented!'

'Hmm,' said Great-Grandma. 'Well she can stay if she must, but I wish that awful man would go away...what's he doing here, anyway?'

This drew a stifled laugh from Elsie – and Rorie had to force herself to keep a straight face.

Uncle Harris's face darkened fleetingly, then he attempted to make light of it. 'Oh, Grandma, you've lost none of your caustic wit! I just thought I'd bring along Arran's two daughters because they are staying with us. You see, we have some rather bad news; Arran's gone missing.'

'Missing? Oh, the silly boy, has he run off again? I remember the last time that happened. Nobody could find him...turned out he was hiding in the wardrobe all the time! Ha ha ha!' Grandma's gravelly laugh gave way to a coughing fit. When she had calmed down, she added, 'Have you checked the wardrobe?'

Rorie bit her lip. She didn't know which way to look.

'Grandma, he's not a six-year-old any more,' said Uncle Harris. 'He's a grown man; these are his children.'

Elsie pulled out the picture of Dad she carried around with her, and showed it to Great-Grandma. 'Oh, *him*!' said the old lady. 'Oh, and he's so lovely to me...he comes to see me, you know, not like you—'

'Both Arran and his wife are missing,' interrupted Uncle Harris. 'So—'

'Both? Did you say both?'

'They've only got amneezer,' said Elsie, pocketing the picture. 'That means you forget who you are. They'll remember soon.'

'Oh, the poor souls! Well, these girls must have someone to look after them. Something must be done! Immediately!'

'It's all right, Grandma; they're staying with us,' said Uncle Harris, patting her vein-wormed hand. 'I just thought you'd want to know that. Everything's being taken care of; you needn't worry.'

Rorie was beginning to feel distinctly uneasy; why did he need to mention their parents' disappearance at all? Surely it would have been kinder not to let the old lady know. She watched Uncle Harris's expression, with its strange air of exaggerated kindness as he went on nodding and patting for rather longer than seemed necessary. Something about this whole visit felt deeply wrong, but she couldn't put her finger on what it was.

'Poor Arran; I wonder where he's got to,' said Great-Grandma. 'Such a naughty boy, but so clever. Mrs Dawkins over there, she's lost her daughter for good, you know...she'll never get over it. Worst thing that can ever happen to a mother, outliving her children. I should know...'

Rorie knew this was a reference to Great-Grandma's daughter – her own Granny. Looking into the watery eyes of this ancient lady – who until now might just as well have been a complete stranger, for all that she felt connected to her – Rorie felt a huge rush of sympathy.

At that moment, a staff nurse approached Uncle Harris. 'Mr Lister is here, sir.'

Uncle Harris stood up immediately. 'Ah, very good...well, girls, say goodbye to your Great-Grandma. Go and wait for me in the waiting room.'

The pretty young nurse indicated for the girls to follow her.

'Goodbye, Great-Grandma,' said Rorie, putting her arms around the old lady. She felt tiny and bird-like in her embrace.

'G'bye,' mumbled Elsie, staring at the floor.

They were about to leave, when Great-Grandma grabbed Rorie's arm and pulled her towards her. 'You'll find him, you know. You will!' And she winked at her.

They followed the nurse out of the communal lounge. 'How'd she know that?' whispered Elsie.

'Well, she doesn't really,' said Rorie. 'Nobody does. I don't know, maybe she's just completely bats; I can't tell.'

'I think she *isn't* bats,' said Elsie firmly. 'She can't be, 'cause everything she says is true; it's just stuff other people wouldn't say.'

'But...all that confusion over who's who...'

'She puts it on, you know,' whispered the nurse as she held open the door. 'It's a game she plays; she knows what's what.' She tapped the side of her nose.

Rorie was tickled by this, until she had a thought. 'Why doesn't our dad bring us here, then?'

'Because he knows how she is when she gets one of

her Black Moods,' said the nurse. 'They can strike at any time, you see; *he* has the sense to protect you from that, ahem. Fortunately, she's OK at the moment.'

The nurse left. The waiting room was empty except for a very young, very bored-looking doorman slumped in his chair, watching the Watersports Channel and not paying much attention to the monitors.

'Oh Elsie,' said Rorie loudly, nudging her and giving her a meaningful look. 'I left that, uh, *book* in the car…I'm just going to get it.'

Elsie's eyes widened in surprise. 'Oh…OK, I'll come with you.'

Rorie turned to the doorman. 'We'll be right back.'

The doorman barely glanced up from his surfers. 'OK.'

Outside, Rorie grabbed Elsie's hand and steered her around the side of the building.

'We gonna excape?' asked Elsie in a loud whisper.

'No!' hissed Rorie. 'Now *shush*! Not a word.'

They crept among the aloes and palm plants along the side of the building. Rorie looked for the large yucca she'd noticed outside the window where Great-Grandma was seated, and made her way toward it. As she did, she could hear loud voices coming from within. Rorie edged close to the open window.

'...Where's Philip?' Great-Grandma was saying. 'I must have Philip here...and Tony. I never pass any laws without my Prime Minister present!'

'Grandma, all you need to do is—' came Uncle Harris's voice.

'Down, Brandy, down!' interrupted the old lady. 'Sarah, do take the corgis out, I think they want feeding.'

Rorie suppressed a laugh as she realised Great-Grandma was pretending she thought she was Queen Elizabeth II.

At the same time there was muffled talk between Uncle Harris and Mr Lister. Rorie couldn't catch all of it, just snippets. 'I thought you said she understood...' 'She does, I can assure you...Don't understand why...' 'I'm sorry, Mr Silk, but it's against Law Society regulations to...' 'Look, she was perfectly lucid just now...maybe it's the effect of some medication...' 'Well, I'm sorry, but...' '...Ask the nurses, they know!' '...Must have a first-hand account...'

Meanwhile Great-Grandma continued to bang on about 'Philip' and 'Tony' and 'the corgis', and becoming increasingly agitated. 'I WON'T PASS ANY LAWS WITHOUT TONY PRESENT!' she screeched, and now Rorie heard the familiar Irish lilt of the staff nurse, 'I'm very sorry, sirs, but you'll have to leave. We can't have Mrs Silk getting upset, it's bad for her heart...there there, Mrs Silk, I've got your medicine here, love.'

'There! You see?' came Uncle Harris's voice, an octave higher than usual. 'They're drugging her...no wonder she's not making any sense!'

'Mr Silk, will you please leave the premises now!' demanded the staff nurse angrily.

'All right, all right,' said Uncle Harris. There was a pause. 'Well, uh, we'll see each other very soon, dearest,' he said in a most conciliatory tone.

'Bog off,' said Great-Grandma.

'Ha ha!' laughed Uncle Harris. 'Still got that mischievous sense of humour!'

Chapter 9
Puzzle

'Complete waste of time,' muttered Mr Lister irritably on his Shel, as he strode out through the reception area. 'Yup. Be back as soon as I can.'

Rorie and Elsie huddled close to the sliding door from which he had just emerged. 'OK; Uncle Harris'll be out any minute,' whispered Rorie, unheard by the lawyer or the receptionist over the TV noises. 'Do it when I nudge, OK?'

Just seconds later, Uncle Harris approached the sliding door while stuffing papers back into his file. Rorie nudged Elsie, who promptly spilt a display box of leaflets onto the highly polished floor.

'Whooaa!' went Uncle Harris, as he slid on the leaflets and went belly up.

Rorie rushed up to him. 'Oh, Uncle Harris, are you all right?' Just as she had hoped, his papers had spilled out of the file; she gathered them up for him. The main item was a folder, which said on the front:

THE LAST WILL

AND

TESTAMENT

OF

LILY SILK

(AMENDED)

At the bottom it read: Lister & Co, Solicitors, Butehurst.

Uncle Harris stood up and brushed himself down. 'Making trouble already!' he barked at Elsie.

'I'm sorry, I didn't mean to, it just—'

'Typical!' he snapped.

Meanwhile, Rorie was shuffling the papers in order, just catching sight of the wording on another one before Uncle Harris snatched the whole lot from her. 'Can't leave you alone for five minutes, can I?'

So *much for his making an effort to get along with us*, thought Rorie.

When they arrived back at Poker Bute Hall, Pat Dry was standing by the entrance, talking to a young man dressed in gardening clothes.

'Rorie, Elsie!' she cried, as she rushed up to embrace them both, much to Uncle Harris's distaste. 'How *are* you, my lovelies? Did you enjoy your trip?'

'It was stinky,' said Elsie.

'Oh, very good, thanks,' said Rorie, nudging her sister.

'This is my son, Luke,' said Pat, as the young man stepped forward.

'Hi,' said Luke shyly, raising a hand in a casual half-wave. Unlike his mother he was slim, with dark, shoulder-length hair, which he wore tucked behind the ears. His cheeks were dry and wind-reddened.

'Mr Silk, could I have a quick word with you?' said Pat, taking him aside.

Rorie stared at them, her heart racing; was there some news about Mum and Dad?

'Psst!' said Luke.

Rorie and Elsie turned.

Luke beckoned them over. 'He's all right, you know,' he muttered under his breath.

'Who?' asked Elsie. 'Dad?'

Luke glanced furtively at his mother and the head teacher. 'No – I mean, I don't know; there's no news. She's just distracting him, so I could let you know

Arthur Clarkson's OK.'

'Oh!'

'Ssh!' hissed Luke. 'I'm looking after him. Found him some nice grubs today.'

'Oh, thank you!' whispered Rorie. 'You're very kind.'

'Nah! I like 'im,' said Luke. He paused as Uncle Harris glanced over. 'He's bloomin' hilarious, actually. Gave me a right old colour display just now!'

'Yesss!' said Rorie under her breath. 'That means he's happy again!'

'All right,' said Luke. 'Better go; don't want old Stick-Face getting suspicious...oh, and by the way, you know them security cameras? Well, the people as watches them don't always pay much attention...specially after seven on week nights.' He gave Elsie a conspiratorial wink and prodded his chest, implying that *he* was the one who didn't "pay much attention".

'All right, off you go,' he added. 'And don't look too happy; we were talking about the school, OK?'

As they crunched across the gravel back to the school entrance, Elsie whispered to Rorie, 'How'd he know I wanted to excape?'

'What?!' hissed Rorie. 'Else, he doesn't mean he's

90

going to let you *run away*, you idiot! He's just letting you know when you might be able to...explore a bit. And by the way, you'd still have to get people to cover for you.' Rorie found herself wishing Luke hadn't mentioned his security duty; he didn't know what a wild card Elsie was. 'Don't you dare do anything stupid, you hear?'

'I hear,' groaned Elsie.

Hammerball, Rorie discovered that afternoon, was played with a modern version of the torture instruments she'd seen on Uncle Harris's study wall. And it was complicated; Rorie couldn't remember the last time she'd been so humiliated. The humiliation continued well after the lesson was over.

'Hey, Rorie!' called Joyce from the other end of the dinner table. 'Great playing today. Remind me to get some falling-over and own-goal lessons from you some time, ha ha!' Several other girls laughed uproariously.

Stumped for a response, Rorie looked away, face aflame.

'Oh, Joyce!' said Moll, who had heard this as she passed by with her tray. 'Remind me; what's rule number 245 in the hammerball rulebook? Is it the one about when to pruntle the wickshaft, or is it the one that tells you how to hold your hammer in a frimptattle?'

Now Joyce was speechless. 'Well, its…it's—'

'You don't know, do you?' said Moll. 'No, thought not.'

At that moment, Aunt Irmine appeared. 'Moll!' she spat, pronouncing it "Mole". 'Victimising poor Joyce again, I see.' She yanked the food tray out of Moll's hands. 'Right, for that, there'll be no dinner for you. To the kitchen, *now*; you'll help with the dishes.'

Rorie jumped up. 'No, please – you've got it all wrong—'

'*Don't* you presume to tell me what's right and what's wrong, young lady!' snapped Aunt Irmine. Then she took Moll by one of her braids and actually pulled her by the hair, off to the kitchen.

Rorie found she had no appetite. She got up to leave, but was soon approached by Alison Clingfilm. 'Don't get involved,' she said gravely. 'Moll's bad news, Rorie.'

'Why?' asked Rorie.

'She's just weird. How she's still here, I don't know!' said Alison. 'All those *things* she insists on wearing in her hair? Ugh. She's permanently on detention, doesn't even share a dorm with the rest of us; she has to stay in a separate room.'

'So...she's never actually done anything *bad*?' asked Rorie. 'Like disrupting class, victimising people, that kind of thing?'

Alison sighed, smiling at her. 'Oh Rorie! You really shouldn't worry about her. You're not that sort of person; I can tell! You're a *good* sort.' She punched Rorie gently on the shoulder, and they each went along their way.

A "*good sort*"? thought Rorie, irritated. *What did that* mean, *for heaven's sake? All power to you, Moll, for taking a stand!*

'Hey, what happened to you?' asked Elsie, trotting over to join her. 'Your eye's all red and fat.'

'And my arm's killing me,' said Rorie. 'When you get a Hammerball lesson, I suggest you throw a sickie; I've never known such a vicious game. Come, we need to talk.' She led Elsie out of the refectory. There was a security camera in the hall; she turned her back to it. 'All right, I give us about one minute here before someone butts in, so here goes: did you understand what was going on back there at the old people's home?'

'What, apart from Great-Grandma acting bonkers?'

'I figured it out,' whispered Rorie, huddling closer. 'Great-Grandma must be leaving all her money to Dad in her will. But Uncle Harris was trying to get her to change it.'

Elsie gasped. 'So *he'd* get all the money instead?'

Rorie nodded, unable to speak for a moment. She found she was trembling.

Elsie's face was like thunder. 'How'd you know?'

'Because he brought an amended will; that's what I picked up when he fell over.'

'How dare he! Is she mega-rich, then?'

'I guess…it's not really the sort of thing Dad talks about.'

'Well anyway, it doesn't matter, 'cause Great-Grandma *din't* sign it,' Elsie pointed out.

'Apparently not.'

'An' she won't never.'

Rorie sighed. 'I hope you're right. What I've been trying to figure out is, why did he need to bring us along? He had us there for a *reason*…'

'Maybe he thought she'd like us better than him,' suggested Elsie.

Rorie rolled her eyes. 'Oh, *right*. How on earth would that help? This is *him* we're talking about, not—' She paused, staring blankly.

Elsie glanced around. 'What?'

Rorie snapped her fingers. 'That's it...of course!'

Elsie jiggled impatiently. '*What*?'

Rorie grabbed her by the shoulders. 'There was another document, some kind of "Certificate of Residence" he was carrying – you know, proving that we live with him. He must have been using that to try to convince Great-Grandma to change her mind. Don't you see? It explains why he dragged us here, even though he doesn't like us! He didn't *have* to – we could have gone to a foster home. But as our legal guardian in place of Mum and Dad, he stands to make money out of us!'

'OK, so like I said; we run away,' said Elsie.

'Else, we *can't*...I mean, don't think I haven't thought of that too, but...well, then what?'

'Then we're gonna find Mum and Dad. They're still alive, I just know it!'

'Look. First off, do you know how isolated we are here? You heard what Uncle Harris said; there's 700 acres of land around the school. Then there's only farmland for ages, before you get to the town.'

'I don't—'

'Anyway, I don't see what good it's going to do just running off like that. What if Mum and Dad are found, and no one knows how to get in touch with us?'

Elsie's eyes filled with tears. 'But *we'd* find them! We can do it better'n anyone can!'

'Else, we haven't any money...we'd have to persuade someone to hide us...it's impossible! Look, let me think a bit more about what to do. But don't go doing anything crazy! And who knows? Maybe Mum and Dad will come back soon.'

Chapter 10
Orchids

Elsie thought she might just go out of her mind with boredom, stuck in the common room with her No. 1 enemy Leesa Simms and no entertainment but boring old puzzles and stuffy old books. Lessons had been excruciating, and there was only one thing she wanted to do now: dress-up. Which wasn't possible. Unless…Elsie suddenly remembered what Luke had said about the cameras 'not paying much attention' after seven o'clock on week nights. Who knew what she might find if she was free to explore? She wondered if it was seven yet, but the clock said 18:45, and she was none the wiser. 'Um, what time is it?' she asked Leesa.

There were cackles of derision. Leesa sighed melodramatically. 'It's a quarter to seven. Don't they teach you *anything* at that other school of yours?'

'Yes!' Elsie snapped angrily. 'They teach you how to not be horrid to each other! And how to make dinosaurs, and write stories, and—'

'Shut up.'

'...They actually *want* you to make stuff up, they *like* it, and—'

'I SAID SHUT UP!!'

Elsie shut up.

'Thank you,' said Leesa Simms. 'Right. That'll be one more demerit; next time it's detention, Elsa Silk.'

Fifteen minutes to go. Elsie tried to escape into some drawing, though she was dismayed with the tiny notepad and one lead pencil she was limited to. She liked making up silly fashions, which was something of a speciality of hers; last year she had won first prize in a school costume competition for Most Original Design for her 'Elsie Sandwich', which was exactly that.

She began vigorously sharpening the pencil, which was the old-fashioned kind, becoming engrossed in seeing just how steely-thin she could get it. She watched as curl after curl of paper-thin wood fell into her lap; she liked the way they resembled the flounces of a skirt. She tried to draw one, but couldn't get it right. She wished she had a gigantic pencil, the size of herself, and a massive sharpener. Wouldn't that be great! In Mum's collection of old *Vogue* magazines there had been something called a pencil skirt – a name she had especially liked.

The moment the clock turned to 19:00, Elsie knew it was time. 'Please Leesa?' she said. 'I need the loo.'

'Well, you're not going alone,' snapped Leesa.

'I'll go with her,' offered one of the girls eagerly.

'All right,' said Leesa; Elsie reluctantly went with the girl. She waited until she was locked in a cubicle, then took her shoes off and crept out.

The corridor was poky and narrow, punctuated with twists and turns. Elsie slipped into the dorm and retrieved the craft box she had brought from home, then headed down some steps, which creaked alarmingly. She glimpsed a Perfect rounding a corner up ahead; she tried to open the nearest door, but it was locked...then she came to a glass door which led down another corridor, and swung through that. She ran as fast as she could. Every door she tried was locked. Finally – at last! – a door at the very end stood ajar; Elsie dived in. The door creaked shut, as if by itself, and she was in total darkness. Elsie let out a whimper; shaking, she felt for the handle...nothing could have prepared her for what happened next.

She was grabbed from behind, and a hand clamped over her mouth.

'What are you doing here?' hissed a girl's voice.

'Mfffmmf!' was all Elsie could reply. Her eyes frantically searched, but there was nothing but pitch black all around.

'OK, just nod when I've got the right gang. Incogz? Leet? Beegox?'

Elsie shook her head at each one.

'Huh. OK, I'm gonna let go, but you're not to yell, or there'll be hell to pay.'

Elsie felt the hand slip away; she did as she was told, but started when a light shone in her face. 'Aah!'

'Ssh!' hissed the girl. 'I told you to be quiet!' Elsie could now make out a pale face, framed by dark hair heavily embellished with decorations. The girl frowned. 'You're new. When did you get here?'

'Yesterday.'

The pale girl sighed with relief. 'OK, that explains it. Lost, I guess. Funny, I just met another girl who arrived yesterday.'

'Rorie?'

'Yeah! How'd you know?'

'I'm her sister, Elsie.'

'*Ah*. You're OK then. I'm Moll.'

Elsie relaxed a little. 'What's all those gangs you were talking about?'

'Oh, guess you wouldn't know,' said Moll, briefly peering out of the closet. 'The Perfects; they all have their teams of snitches who snoop around for them, weeding out anyone who doesn't conform. All right, off you go, scram – but you didn't see me, OK?'

'But I don't *want* to go back there!' protested Elsie. 'I was looking for dress-up things. Can you help me?'

Moll gave her a sideways look, then smiled. 'Well…all right. Come on.' She checked again that all was clear, then led Elsie out into the hallway. 'Don't worry about the security cameras,' she whispered. 'I'm very good at dodging them.'

'Oh, my friend Luke says I can go where I like, anyway,' said Elsie. 'He's Not Looking.' She gave an exaggerated wink, imitating the one Luke gave her.

Moll raised her eyebrows. 'Really? That's handy. OK, through here.' She punched out a code on the keypad beside a door, and they went in. She led Elsie in and out of classrooms, and a chemistry lab, where she helped herself to some gloves and tools.

'What're you doing?' asked Elsie.

'You'll see.'

Then down a back staircase, past the school kitchen

and down more stairs, which led to the basement.

Elsie felt her heart quicken; she associated wonderful things with basements.

'Treasure trove!' said Moll, wheeling one of the large recycling bins toward her. 'Old uniforms in here,' – she pulled out another one – 'mufti in here. Take your pick.'

'Hey, thanks!' Elsie delved eagerly into the 'mufti' box; in it were mostly old T-shirts, slants and sweaters. 'Hmm...not very dress-uppy.'

'Yeah, but you could *make* something, like I do,' suggested Moll, pulling on the gloves. She took an aluminium food container from another bin and began cutting it with one of the tools. 'I make jewellery out of this stuff.'

'The things in your hair?'

'Yup, all my own work,' Moll grinned mischievously. 'I like freaking Mr Silk out; he has *no idea* how I keep getting more of these things every time he confiscates them. It's hilarious!'

Inspired, Elsie took her scissors out and enjoyed hacking at one of the loathed school uniform shirts. She liked the way the collar was so sculptural; it reminded her of a crisp, white version of the pencil shavings. She hummed happily to herself as she sliced the collars off several more shirts. 'I'm gonna make a wedding dress,' she declared.

'Great idea!' said Moll, as she moulded little pieces of aluminium. 'I'll make you a bracelet to go with it.'

'Yeah!' breathed Elsie excitedly. Now nothing else existed: not her worries about Mum and Dad, not even Poker Bute Hall. Just her and Moll, in this moment, making things. 'You can be my new best friend if you like,' she declared. 'I don't mind that you're too old.'

Moll laughed. 'Well, thanks! But you're not to tell anyone about this; it's our secret.'

'Oh, cross my heart and hope to die!' vowed Elsie, as she began sticking the collars together with her fabric glue, forming a layered skirt. 'So now we're best friends, you have to tell me how you figure out those codes.'

'Uh-uh!' said Moll. 'Not telling. But tell me about you; how come you moved in the middle of the year?'

As Elsie finished off her wedding dress, she explained all about what had happened with Mum and Dad. Somehow it didn't make her upset; she was telling a story – exaggerating here and there – and it was as if she was talking about someone else's life. Then she asked Moll to tell her more about the Gangs of Poker Bute Hall. 'There must be *some* real gangs, aren't there?'

'Sorry to disappoint you,' said Moll. 'Nothing but snitches. But I'm always one step ahead of them, ha ha!'

'Ha ha!' echoed Elsie, copying Moll's mannerisms exactly, as she always did with people she admired. 'Well, *we* could start a gang,' she suggested, stepping into her dress.

Moll chuckled, as she helped Elsie tie up the halter-style top of the dress. 'We could call it "The Orchids".

Elsie frowned. 'Why?'

'That's the flower on your bracelet. Oh hey – even better...here.' Moll removed her own necklace from under her shirt and placed it around Elsie's neck. It had the same flower on it. 'You want to know what's great about orchids? They don't follow the rules. There's like, a gazillion different species; there are always some kinds becoming extinct – yet hundreds of new species are discovered every year. You want to know what I think?'

'What?'

Moll moved closer, her eyes bright. 'I think they're the *same ones*, only dressed differently. They won't allow themselves to be classified. That's what I'm like

104

– and that's why they hate me here. You're the same, I can tell.' She held up a large sheet of aluminium, as a makeshift mirror. 'OK, give us a twirl.'

Elsie studied her rather warped reflection, turning this way and that. 'Wow! I look like a proper bride.' And she paraded around, singing, 'Here comes the bride, all fat and wide, see how she waddles from side to-o side!'

'Ssh!' hissed Moll suddenly. 'I think – oh boy – someone's coming.'

Elsie heard muffled sounds like faint footsteps.

'Quick, I know a way out back here,' urged Moll. She helped Elsie gather up her things and headed toward the other end of the basement.

Elsie hurried after her. Moll clambered up onto another recycling bin, and up into the disposal chute above it. Elsie, too, wedged herself into the narrow tunnel and began shuffling her way up it, with only the thin ridges of its steel panels to grip onto. But the glue on her makeshift dress hadn't had time to bond; the thing was falling apart. A piece of Poker Bute Hall shirt collar fell away and she trod on it and slipped. 'Aah!' she cried, as she fell down and landed in a heap on a pile of papers.

And there, standing over her, was Uncle Harris.

Chapter 11
Pretty Rosy Face

Rorie was sitting alone in her window seat in the common room, pretending to read. In fact, she was lost in her thoughts about Mum and Dad. She was haunted by the image of that speeding car from Inspector Dixon's Shel. 11:21, the time counter had recorded; running late. Perhaps they *had* returned home to get something, been delayed somehow...but surely they were still alive somewhere. They *had* to be.

Her thoughts were interrupted by Moll, who had slipped into the common room so stealthily, no one seemed to notice. 'Oh!' Rorie jumped, startled. 'Oh, it's you...sorry, I was miles away.' She peered at Moll, who looked bedraggled. 'Hey, is something up?'

'Oh, no, nothing; how are you?' said Moll breezily, but something about the way she said it – a little too loud, a little forced – suggested to Rorie she was putting on an act. 'What are you reading?' she asked, putting her hand up to the ebook Rorie was holding. As she did so, she slipped a small, folded piece of paper into her hand.

'Oh…it's, uh, just some geodata prep,' said Rorie. Now she understood; Moll had a secret message for her.

'Best of luck,' said Moll, squeezing her hand and giving Rorie a rather intense stare. 'I really hope everything works out for you.' Then she left the room.

Rorie gazed at her retreating figure, perplexed. *It's only homework*! she thought. Burning with curiosity, she opened out the piece of paper, hiding it behind the ebook. She read:

Rorie: Elsie's got detention. They're making her do work in the garden. Now, in the dark – it's freezing out there. See if you can get to her somehow. Kitchen garden, just outside the refectory.

Moll

Crushing the piece of paper, Rorie checked the time; half an hour to go till bedtime drill. With Luke manning the security cameras, she didn't have to worry about being reported for prowling – as long as she could avoid being seen by anyone else. She slipped out of the common room.

Once out of the building, Rorie ran all the way to the kitchen garden. It was a grim night; dark, undulating layers of cloud boiled overhead, and the birdless treetops flailed restlessly. Poor Elsie! What on earth could she have done to deserve being made to work out here on this cold, dark February evening? Especially with all the anguish she was going through right now.

Approaching the garden, Rorie caught sight of Elsie, eerily lit by floodlights, but she appeared to be alone; a forlorn little figure, sitting cross-legged on the ground. As Rorie drew nearer, she could see that Elsie seemed to be eating something from a small packet.

'Elsie!' she called, dashing to her side.

Elsie looked up; her face was smeared with grime where she had wiped away tears with grubby hands. She said nothing, and went back to what she was doing. Rorie watched, bewildered, as Elsie now took some of the contents of the small packet – it looked like flower seeds – and shoved them up her nose.

'What on earth are you doing?' asked Rorie.

Elsie just frowned, shook her head, then shut her eyes, hands resting on her knees.

'Elsie!' pleaded Rorie, shaking her by the shoulders.

Elsie coughed, and a globule of spit-covered seeds spluttered out. '*Guh*...Rorie! You spoiled my 'speriment!'

'What experiment? Why are you on your own? Surely someone should be supervising you?'

'There was a Perfect, but she's gone,' said Elsie, digging a finger in her ear; more seeds tumbled out. 'She said I'm evil and ugly, so I told her no, *she's* evil and ugly, and this whole stinking *place* is evil. So she said she was sending me to Coventry, so I said "well I bet it's better there than here", and then...she just went away.'

'How long ago was this?'

'Just a bit 'fore you got here.'

Rorie blinked at her. 'Elsie, why were you stuffing seeds into your ears, nose and mouth?'

'I told you, it was a 'speriment. 'Cause I'm fed up of people calling me ugly, an' I wanna be beautiful, like when I do dress up, only I'm not allowed to here...' She paused.

Rorie looked at the picture on the seed packet. '*Roses?*'

Elsie scowled. 'I knew you'd fink it's silly. Well, I'm allowed to do any 'speriment I like, so there. I'm gonna grow a head of flowers; *then* I'll be beautiful.' She reached for the seed packet again; Rorie saw that by her side there was also a bottle of green stuff called 'WonderGrow'.

Rorie snatched the packet out of her hand. 'Elsie, don't be daft; you'd either choke or poison yourself!'

'I *told* you you wouldn't understand!' said Elsie crossly.

Rorie checked herself. 'No, I do, Else,' she said, trying to sound sympathetic. 'At least...I think you're very imaginative. It's not something I'd ever have dreamt of, because I don't have your imagination.'

'You wouldn't need to grow flowers anyway. You don't know what it's like to be ugly,' said Elsie.

'You're not ugly, Else, any more than you're evil,' said Rorie. 'Uncle Harris is evil...*that Perfect is evil*; she should never have left you alone. You might have died!' She shuddered as she realised just how dangerous the situation was. But at the same moment, it occurred to her just what a wonderful opportunity it gave them. 'Else?' she said. 'You know how you were talking yesterday about running away?'

Elsie jumped up. 'Yes?'

'Let's do it. Now.'

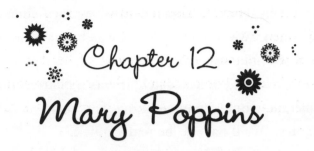

Chapter 12
Mary Poppins

The idea of running away had occurred to Rorie on the spur of the moment, but the more she thought about it, the more she realised they just had to do it. It didn't seem crazy any more. How much more did they have to suffer at this wretched place? As for Mum and Dad – well, if she and Elsie kept an eye on the news, they'd know if they were found. And then – *only* then – they could come forward, be reunited with their parents, and live happily ever after.

'Hey, if we're going, we should take Arthur Clarkson!' said Elsie.

Rorie paused. 'Oh, you're right. But...'

'It's OK, I think I know where he is!'

'Really?'

'Yeah; come on, I'll show you!'

Perched behind a bush, they peered out; nobody

was around. Keeping low, they trotted across the lawns close to the shrubbery, as droplets of rain began to fall. 'In there,' whispered Elsie, as they came to a large shed. 'We passed it when I was brought out here; I fink it's Luke's shed.'

Rorie looked at her watch; it was a quarter to nine. Someone would come looking for them in fifteen minutes. 'We'll have to be really quick.'

Sure enough, they soon found a large cage, and inside it was Arthur Clarkson. He looked pleased to see them; reds and yellows flickered along his scaly back. 'Hello, Arthur!' whispered Elsie.

Rorie reached into the cage and lifted him out. 'Sorry, old man; we're going on another journey.' Looking at Elsie's uniform, she sighed. 'If only we could change our clothes.'

Elsie inspected a moth-eaten sweater.

'Ugh, don't even think about it,' said Rorie. 'Come on, we've got to hurry!'

Elsie picked up a large umbrella. 'OK...but I wanna bring this. It's raining.'

'It's not yours, Else! And Luke's been so kind and helpful—'

'We'll get wet an' die of newmonomia,' insisted Elsie.

Rorie felt herself caving in. They *would* need protection; they had a long way to go. And it was only an umbrella, after all…

If there was one thing Arthur Clarkson didn't like, it was being jostled about. And this time Rorie didn't have anything to carry him in; she just cradled him close to her chest. Already, the chameleon had stopped displaying his sunshine colours and was going into murky mode.

They had no idea where they were going, but instinctively headed for the wooded area beyond the gardens at the back of the school.

Rorie quickened her pace, eager to reach cover. 'How dare they treat you like that! What was it supposed to be for, anyway?'

'I went exploring, 'cause Luke said I could, that's all,' said Elsie. 'Then I met this girl Moll, and we were having a good time in the basement, making stuff. Then Uncle Harris came, but Moll got away an' I didn't. I s'pose she din't know right away I wasn't behind her…but then she came back, saying it was her fault an' they shouldn't punish me.'

'She did? That was really kind of her. She's the one who told me where you were as well. But he still gave you detention.'

'Yeah, and Moll's gone; she's been sent on some special Anger Management course.'

Rorie stopped in her tracks. 'She has? So that's why...'

'Why what?'

'Oh, it's just the way she behaved earlier...boy, I hope she'll be OK.'

Much as Rorie welcomed the cover of the trees, she now felt a shiver of anxiety about what might be lurking in the undergrowth. 'Let's see how fast we can get to the other side,' she said, gathering bravado; together they bounded forth. Rorie soon forgot her fears; just having got this far felt like an immense triumph; every metre further away from the dreadful Poker Bute Hall gave them more hope. Coming out the other side of the wood, with more hills stretching away before them, they thrust themselves forward with abandon. Rorie felt exhilarated as the wind blew through her hair; she had no idea how much further they had to go – probably a long way – but she was determined they would make it. She didn't even care that the weather was growing more turbulent by the minute.

Elsie was tearing away ahead of her, the umbrella

carrying her along as it caught the wind. It was a large umbrella, big enough to shelter them both, but Elsie seemed to have forgotten this. Suddenly a huge gust of wind thrust the umbrella upwards, and little Elsie's feet were actually lifted off the ground for a moment. 'Wheee!' she cried. 'I'm Mary Poppins!'

'Elsie, stop it!' called Rorie, as she stumbled up the hill towards her. The rain was still light, but a flash of lighting signified that there was worse to come.

But Elsie wasn't listening; she giggled as the wind tossed the umbrella this way and that. There was a crash of thunder, and another gust of wind threw her even higher this time, sending her into paroxysms of delight. 'Higher! Higher!' she cried. 'I'm Mary Poppins!'

Realising the storm was worse than she'd thought – and approaching more rapidly – Rorie called out again. 'Elsie! It's not safe!' Clutching Arthur Clarkson for all she was worth, she ran to catch up. 'Elsie, listen to me!'

'I'll give you a go in a minute!' Elsie called back over her shoulder. 'Wheee!'

Rorie reached the brow of the hill, and finally caught up with Elsie. 'Elsie, we can't stay out here!'

'I'm not going back!' snapped Elsie, still skipping

and whirling in the wind. 'No way, José!'

Rorie ran to keep up with her. 'Look, I'm not saying we have to go back, just that we should shelter somewhere…'

'In a while,' said Elsie. 'This is fun! Wheee!'

Furious now, Rorie reached for the umbrella, grasping it by the steel shaft. A split-second later, the umbrella's tip made contact with the heavens and hot white light hurtled down the shaft and into Rorie, sending her shooting into the air with the velocity of cannon-fire…Elsie screamed, instantly releasing the umbrella handle; Rorie was thrown to the ground like a rag doll, and there was an almighty crash of thunder…the rain came pelting down.

Elsie pummelled at her sister's chest, now soaked with rain. 'Wake up, Rorie,' she cried. 'Wake up!'

Arthur Clarkson lay on Rorie's stomach, all his lights gone out. 'Oh no, Arthur!' whispered Elsie, before resuming the thumping. 'Rorie wake up, please! I'm sorry!'

The chameleon slid to the ground, motionless.

Still Elsie shook and pummelled and begged, as rivulets of rain ran down the sides of Rorie's face.

Suddenly Elsie was aware of a soft shaft of light approaching through the rain; she looked up, and seeing Luke's jeep, she ran towards it. 'Help!' she cried, waving her arms about.

'There you are!' yelled Luke, as he drew up. 'I heard you were missing, so I...what the heck?' He jumped down and kneeled beside Rorie. 'Was she struck by lightning?'

'I...there was this *whoosh* and...oh no!' was all Elsie could say. It had all happened too fast for her to make any sense of it.

'Oh my God,' said Luke, dropping to his knees. He picked up Rorie's hand and felt her wrist. After what felt to Elsie like an eternity, he announced, 'She's still alive.' Then he leaned over, held Rorie's head back and clamped his mouth to hers.

Elsie's head was full of questions, none of which she dared ask. She just stood in the rain beside the ripped, smouldering umbrella.

Chapter 13
A Colourful Life

'Oh goodness, look! She's awake!'

Rorie's eyes slowly focused on the white room, then on Pat Dry, who hoved into view. Something somewhere was beeping, and her hands hurt. 'Hi,' she croaked.

'Rorie! You OK?' came Elsie's voice.

Rorie looked around, and found her. 'Elsie? What's the matter? Where am I?'

Elsie looked amazed. 'Don't you remember?'

'Oh, she's had a terrible shock, dear,' said Pat Dry. She turned to Rorie. 'How are you feeling? It's all right, I've called the doctor; he'll be along in a minute...'

Rorie propped herself up on her elbows. 'What shock? What happened?'

'You were struck by lightning, dear.'

As soon as she heard the words, Rorie saw again

her right hand reaching for the umbrella shaft, felt the thump that whacked its way into the very core of her being.

'...Your name, sweetie?' Pat was saying.

'What?'

'Do you remember your name?'

'Well, of course I do—'

'What is it?'

'Rorie Silk, but—'

'Well, thank heaven for that!' said Pat. 'Sometimes they get amnesia, you know; that's what the doctor said.'

Amnesia, thought Rorie vaguely. *That reminds me of something*...As her memory began to fill in the blanks, a heavy feeling enveloped her. The words 'Poker Bute Hall' loomed ominously; she would have to go back there. She'd been trying to escape – yes, that was it – she and Elsie. *Elsie with her stupid umbrella, and me with*...

'Where's Arthur Clarkson?' she asked suddenly.

Pat and Elsie looked at each other, and their expression told Rorie all she needed to know. 'Oh, poor Arthur!' She began to cry.

'It was very quick, love,' said Pat. 'He wouldn't have known a thing. The lightning bolt travelled through the umbrella shaft, through you, and then into poor old Arthur. Too much for the little chap to take, I'm afraid.'

'We haven't buried him yet,' added Elsie. 'We were waiting for you.'

Rorie was struck by how matter-of-fact Elsie was about Arthur's death. But then, having just watched her sister nearly get fried to a crisp must have been a great deal worse. Rorie stared at her hands and frowned; they were bandaged, and a device like a big watch was strapped to her right wrist.

'You have burns at the entry and exit points,' explained Pat. 'It's as if a giant needle has made a stitch through you, from one hand to the other.'

'But Elsie was holding the umbrella as well,' said Rorie, perplexed.

'Ah, but she was protected because she was holding the *handle*,' explained Pat. 'It's insulated.'

'Anyway, now you're awake,' said Elsie, 'we can have Arfur's funeral.'

'Well, if she gets discharged, dear,' added Pat. 'We need to be sure you're OK, Rorie.' She studied the monitor that Rorie now realised was picking up body function information from the wireless device on her wrist. 'Still, you certainly seem to be doing all right.

You're ever so lucky, you know; some people get *incinerated*; just a hollow shell of a person left behind. Or else they—'

'Pat!' snapped Rorie.

'Oh! Me and my big mouth,' said Pat. 'There I go again. Never mind, dear; you're fine, that's the important thing. In fact, if you want my opinion,' she added, moving nearer, 'I'd say there was *divine magic* at work! Ssh! Don't let on to old Stick-Face I said such a thing.'

'What do you mean?' asked Rorie.

'I think it's a *sign*…now, I'm not saying it's the same as with the saints; heaven forbid! But those marks on your hands—'

But she was interrupted by the doctor, who walked in at that moment. 'Ah, Miss Silk! You're awake…how is she doing, Mrs Dry?'

'Right here'll be OK,' said Luke, digging his spade into the ground. 'But let's be quick about it, all right? Old Stick-Face mustn't know, and there are snitches all over this place.' He began shovelling the dirt.

'Thank you, Luke,' said Rorie, cradling the bundled-up dead chameleon in her hands. 'This is very kind of you.'

They had only just returned from the hospital, Rorie having been given the all clear from the doctor; 'although she must have complete rest for a few days,' he had warned. Rorie had been particularly glad to hear about that. And since Uncle Harris and Aunt Irmine were out at a head teacher's convention, they had the perfect opportunity to hold a funeral for the creature who was supposed to have left the premises long ago.

Luke was so good-natured, it made Rorie blush with guilt; she and Elsie had, after all, been trying to run away when the accident happened, and Elsie had already got him into trouble over her wanderings. Rorie wouldn't have blamed him if he'd wanted nothing more to do with them.

He'd refused to take the credit for saving Rorie's life. 'It was Elsie did that,' he'd said, and the doctor had agreed.

'If someone dies from a lightning strike,' the doctor had explained, 'it is cardiac arrest that kills them; the heart stops. Elsie's thumping on your chest could have kick-started it again. But the extra oxygen you got from Luke would certainly have helped you to recover.'

Rorie had blushed at that too, though she didn't remember him giving her the kiss of life. But she was relieved for Elsie's sake that she had something to be proud of; she had been beating herself up over the accident, saying it was all her fault.

'All right,' said Luke, once the hole was dug. 'Got any words you want to say?'

Rorie knelt down with the little bundle – it felt right to wrap the dead chameleon up, somehow. 'Um, well…we'll miss you terribly, Arthur,' she said, though it felt silly.

'Poor Arfur,' added Elsie. 'An' Mum 'n' Dad'll miss you too…er, even if they have got amneezer. I fink…'

'Um…you had four and a half colourful years of life,' said Rorie. 'Very colourful.'

'Four an' a half, you say?' asked Luke.

'Yes.'

'Ah, he was an old man anyway; probably wouldn't have lasted another year. I been readin' up about chameleons; don't usually live more'n five years. Anyhow, you ready to, uh…?'

'Yes,' sniffed Rorie, and she let the bundle slip into the ground.

Elsie instinctively clasped her hands together in prayer and scrunched up her eyes. 'Praise be unto the Father,' she said, 'and unto the Son…and into the hole he goes. Amen.'

'Well, well, well,' said Uncle Harris later that evening, back at the school sickbay. 'That'll teach you to go running off like that, won't it, hmm?'

'The grass isn't always greener on the other side, you know,' added Aunt Irmine, shaking her head knowingly.

But in this case it most certainly is, thought Rorie.

There was a knock at the door.

'Enter!' commanded Uncle Harris, and Inspector Dixon appeared.

Rorie sat up to greet him, eyes searching.

'I heard about the accident,' said Dixon. 'They told me I'd find you here...Rorie, how are you?'

Rorie sighed. 'Tired...very tired.'

Pat held out her hand to Dixon. 'I'm the nurse here; Pat Dry.'

Dixon blinked at her hand.

'That's her *name*,' explained Elsie.

'Oh! Hello,' said the policeman, shaking Pat's hand. 'So, how is the patient doing?'

'She's very lucky,' said Pat. 'Just some numbness in her arm – and she needs a great deal of sleep. The doctor says both things are quite common in such cases. The arm may take several days to return to normal.'

'Mmm…heaven knows what we'll do with *this* one,' moaned Uncle Harris, indicating Elsie. 'Half term, you know,' he explained to Inspector Dixon. 'We'll have to keep her very busy, make sure she stays out of trouble.'

'But I'll need to look after Rorie!' Elsie piped up.

'The poor dears will need to spend some time together,' agreed Pat.

'Yes,' added Dixon. 'The girls have been through an awful lot. And—'

'With respect, officer,' interrupted Uncle Harris sharply. 'You don't know what a *loose cannon* we're dealing with here.'

'With respect, Mr Silk,' Dixon replied, equally sternly. 'I suggest you try to understand just how traumatic this all is for the girls. Now, I have some information for you,' he added, turning to Rorie. 'I'm sorry to have to say that we think your parents may – and I stress, *may* – have been involved in an accident after all.'

Rorie's jaw fell open. 'But I thought you said—'

'One that *hadn't been reported*, because there were no witnesses,' explained Dixon.

Rorie felt as if black curtains were closing in front of her.

'But we have nothing conclusive,' Dixon added

hastily. 'We simply have to consider every possibility…you do understand.'

'Yes, I understand,' said Rorie flatly.

'I wouldn't have wanted to tell you at such a time, but I felt it was better coming from me than if you heard it on the news, or…from someone else.' Dixon glanced at Uncle Harris.

Uncle Harris composed himself, apparently barely able to contain his glee. '*Ahem*. And, ah…*how* is it that there were no witnesses?'

'There was a diversion in place, just north of that speed camera which recorded your brother's car,' Dixon explained. 'The road was closed because of an unstable tunnel…'

'Oh!' cried Rorie. 'You don't mean…'

'The tunnel collapsed.'

'Oh, my word!' cried Pat Dry. She wittered on, but her voice dissolved into thin air as Rorie sat motionless, her head filled with the image of Mum and Dad in the car, fretting about the time…and Dad, never one to obey instructions, doing it his own way. 'It's a much quicker route,' he might have said as he zoomed through the barrier…

Chapter 14
All the Rage

For three days, Rorie existed in a twilight zone between waking and sleeping. She dreamed repeatedly of Mum and Dad appearing – sometimes in Dad's lab, which magically materialised in a Poker Bute Hall classroom ('we've been here all the time!'), sometimes emerging from a pile of rubble. One time, Rorie dreamed she found them under a desk, only five centimetres tall. 'Sorry love,' said Tiny Dad. 'Got a bit lost! Hit the remote, will you?' And Rorie discovered that she had the remote in her hand, and all she had to do was press the right button, and her parents returned to their normal size.

By Wednesday she was able to stay awake most of the day. Her hands were no longer bandaged, but her arm still ached and her palms, scorched in the middle, were still tender.

Still, nothing had been found at the site of the collapsed tunnel. It would take at least another week to clear the site completely; meanwhile the police continued to make enquiries in the area. Rorie had asked to have Internet access over the half term, to keep up with the news, but Uncle Harris had forbidden it. 'Internet access, indeed!' he had scoffed. 'You must think I was born yesterday!'

All the same, they got regular updates from Pat Dry. Every day that passed in which no bodies, no wreckage were found, was a day for celebration. As long as there was hope, Rorie could bear it.

By Thursday she was restless, and her arm had returned to normal. So she was roped in to help Elsie with the pile of mending Aunt Irmine had lumbered her with.

'We are *so* getting out of here,' Rorie muttered under her breath, the moment Aunt Irmine had gone out of the room.

'Yippee! Now?' said Elsie, jumping up.

'No, not yet,' said Rorie, pulling her down. 'Next week. It'll be easier when all the girls are back – and I should be completely back to normal.'

'Mum 'n' Dad might have got over their amneezer by then!' Elsie piped up.

Rorie looked at her. 'Yeah…maybe.' She knew Elsie needed to cling to this idea, but she herself was fast running out of hope. 'But listen, if they don't…'

'Hey, maybe Pat'll help us,' suggested Elsie. 'She's our friend.'

'Are you crazy?' said Rorie. 'Oh. I guess you wouldn't know; Pat *drinks*. Constantly. She's out of her tree all the time. I realised that the first day I was in sickbay. You know that coffee mug she's always slurping from? Fifty per cent coffee; the rest is booze.'

'No!' gasped Elsie. 'So *that's* where that weird smell comes from.'

'Exactly.'

'Wow. Isn't it weird how everyone here's either horrid or mad?'

'Or both,' added Rorie. 'Except for Luke – and he hardly even counts, since he's not actually *in* the school. And the girls are such drones; have you noticed how they all seem to be either geeks or sports freaks?'

'Ha ha, yeah,' laughed Elsie. 'Geeks 'n' Freaks…'

Rorie grabbed her arm. 'I tell you, there's something seriously spooky about it – it's not normal! Moll's the only one who's not like the rest of them, and now she's having to do some ridiculous course…she thought there was something weird going on too. And

Uncle Harris is trying to...oh, here comes Aunt Irmine; We'll discuss it later. We just *have* to figure out a plan to get out of here.'

Rorie didn't know it then, but a plan was soon to present itself in a most unexpected way...

The following Sunday, girls started arriving back at Poker Bute Hall, ready for the second half of the term. Rorie and Elsie were recruited to help serve refreshments for parents who were delivering their daughters.

Elsie pouted. 'Why do we have to do this?' she moaned, trailing behind Rorie as she wheeled out a trolley of biscuits and cakes. 'We're not *servants*.'

'Ssh!' hissed Rorie. 'Well, I don't know about you, but *I'm* dead curious.' They emerged into the hall where the parents were congregating. 'Oh boy, just look at them.'

Elsie surveyed the room. 'They're not a bit like any of Mum and Dad's friends, are they?'

'Why am I not surprised?' said Rorie. 'Come on.' She wheeled the trolley over and started laying things out on the table. Two mums stood nearby, a tall one and a short one. From the way the tall woman posed haughtily in her Victorian-ringlet hair and over-the-knee boots, Rorie guessed this look must be all the rage this week.

'...Never gives me any trouble at all,' the woman was saying to her companion, a rather squat lady who also wore her hair in ringlets, but less successfully. 'She keeps her room so tidy,' the tall woman went on, 'and I'm glad to say that all that nonsense with the music has stopped since she's been coming here.' Rorie didn't know whose mother she was, but she might have been talking about absolutely any Poker Bute Hall girl, except for Elsie, Moll and herself. Every now and then, the squat lady would nod eagerly, saying, 'Mmm, Diandra too...yes!'

Rorie took her time setting everything out, as a father joined the two women. His Victorian-gent style mutton-chop whiskers complemented the ladies' ringlets. 'Just been talking to Mr Silk,' he said. 'He's absolutely convinced me I did the right thing in investing in Tramlawn Schools. They're the only ones that really understand the lesson learned from the millennium crisis, you see.'

'Mmm, mmm, absolutely,' chorused the two women.

'I mean, for forty years, children were given more and more freedom,' Mutton-Chops went on, 'and look where it got us. People were actually *afraid* of their children; didn't know how to tell them what to do!'

'Mmm, mmm, absolutely,' chorused the two women.

'No, the only way to keep the little monsters under control is *fear*. They get the right sort of history lessons here, I can tell you.'

'Mmm, mmm, absolutely,' chorused the two women.

'Aurora!' snapped Aunt Irmine, suddenly appearing at Rorie's side. 'There are people over there who haven't been served yet!'

Rorie instantly busied herself. 'Oh, yes, of course.'

Uncle Harris looked all puffed up with pride; her curiosity was aroused. '...Whole wing that could be redeveloped,' he was saying. 'We could take in boys! Yes...that's my ambition. Tramlawn have no plans as yet. But one could always take over...'

So *that's what he's up to*! thought Rorie, edging nearer.

Uncle Harris spotted her, and his ears twitched nervously. '...Make, make over,' he corrected hastily, to confused looks.

'*If* the money were available,' pointed out one mother.

Quite, thought Rorie. And we all know where he thinks he's going to get it from.

'Er...yes. So, to summarise, in essence, the point I was making earlier,' added Uncle Harris quickly, 'we give many examples of societies where so-called "freedom of expression" has only led to trouble, throughout the ages...'

'If only *all* schools were like this,' said a mother, taking a biscuit from the plate offered by Rorie.

Thank heaven they're not, thought Rorie, as she walked away. Although if people like Uncle Harris got their way, they would be...

Chapter 15
Caroline's Shirt

'Clangalangalangg!!' went the bell the next morning. Like a robot, Rorie roused herself along with all eight other girls in the dorm – the ninth, Alison Clingfilm, was suffering from flu, so had not returned yet. Rorie opened her locker, and saw that she had no shirts.

Joyce, whose locker was next to hers, noticed Rorie standing and staring. 'What's the matter?' she asked brusquely.

'Nothing,' was Rorie's immediate reaction, then she admitted, 'It's just that my shirts aren't back from the laundry yet.'

'Well, did you *send* them?'

Rorie shrugged. 'I put them in my laundry bag.'

'Well, hello?' said Joyce sarcastically. 'It's not going to walk there by itself, is it?' Titter, titter, went the other girls. 'Laundry's collected every Tuesday and

Saturday from outside the dorm,' explained Joyce, rolling her eyes. 'It's in the rules.'

'Well, nobody *told* me!' replied Rorie between gritted teeth. She sighed and pulled one of her used shirts out of the laundry bag. *Yuck*; it was crumpled and grimy, and smelled of used tights. The other shirt was even worse; it was the one she'd worn the day of the lightning strike. She had worn her own clothes since then – mostly pyjamas – and had been too spaced out to ask about the laundry. What was she going to do? Now she wished Alison Clingfilm was around; *she* would have been only too glad to lend her a shirt. Rorie would have to ask someone else...anybody but Joyce. 'Um, Caroline? Would you have a spare shirt I could borrow?'

'Well, I suppose so,' said Caroline, who was the one who'd giggled at Rorie's name. 'But please don't get any marks on it; I got a star last term for best-kept uniform.'

Rorie took the shirt gratefully. 'Oh thank you! I promise I'll keep it nice and clean!'

She began to put it on.

'Oh, but don't forget!' said Caroline, grinning patronisingly as she wagged her finger. 'Games kit first, for Housework Duty, ha ha!'

'Oh yes,' said Rorie. 'Ha ha.'

Rorie was still fumbling with her cravat after assembly; Caroline's shirt was even stiffer than her own, so much so that it was reluctant to close itself around her neck, preferring to jut out in front of her, engulfing her chin and causing the cravat to come undone. There was probably some secret way of dealing with this problem, but Rorie didn't feel like asking, only to get more belittling comments like, 'Haven't you figured it out yet?' or, 'You should have read the rules properly.' With Moll and Alison Clingfilm away, she felt quite isolated; everyone else was either hostile, like Joyce, or organised into close-knit groups like the Carolines. Even though she hardly knew Moll, she missed her and wondered when she might return.

Still fumbling, Rorie consulted her timetable to see what the first lesson was: 'I.S.' What *was* I.S.? She knew it wasn't the same as I.T....then she noticed that the others were already on their way to the I.S. room, and quickly gathered up her things; she'd have to keep up, or she'd never find her way there.

Miss Pretty was a vulture-like woman with a disconcerting squint. 'Right, now, your information storage assignment for this morning will be to write about what you did over half term...'

Information storage? Glancing surreptitiously at her timetable again, Rorie noticed there were no lessons called 'English' – but a lot of 'I.S.' ones. She guessed that this was what 'English' had been reduced to in this place where there was just 'One Right Way" to do anything, and poetry, laughter and drama were scorned upon.

'...And *try* to stick to the facts,' Miss Pretty instructed bossily. 'Some of you have a tendency to stray from the point. I'm afraid it really isn't useful for me to know about the ghost you imagined might be in your cousin's house; if it didn't happen, don't mention it.'

Rorie couldn't think of anything more thrilling than a ghost story – who cared whether it was real or not? – and her heart sank as she realised that she had absolutely nothing to say about her own half term.

She stared blankly at the page. She could hardly tell the truth: that she'd been struck by lightning while trying to run away, and spent most of the rest of the week in bed. She considered writing that, like Alison, she'd caught a particularly nasty flu bug, but rapidly went off that idea; she'd still be stuck with describing her week in sickbay, and what was there to say about that? That Pat Dry spent the whole time getting drunk?

Oh, it's so unfair! she thought. The exercise only served as a painful reminder of the fact that, unlike everyone else in the room, *she* had had to spend the whole week at Poker Bute Hall, instead of with her family, because her parents were missing.

'Aurora,' said Miss Pretty. 'Is something the matter?'

'Oh, no Miss.'

'Then please get on with your piece.'

'Yes, Miss.' Rorie just began writing something, anything:

La la la la la la la

was how it began. But eventually, words started to form:

la la la last week I visited my grandparents in Dorset. There are stables near them, so I was able to go riding. The horse I rode was a two-year-old bay, and she was very well behaved.

What on earth is all this tosh? thought Rorie. She guessed she must be making it up, yet it wasn't the sort of thing she would have invented. Even her handwriting seemed to have magically become neater.

138

She carried on anyway, figuring she might as well tell the whole story, whatever it was, since she had no real story to tell. On and on she wrote: about the two-year-old bay, about the exact location of the stables, the other horses, etc. Next she described some fossils in great detail, cataloguing them one after another, then went on to do exactly the same with a series of meals she'd supposedly had.

Finally Rorie put her pen down, confident that she had produced the sort of work that Poker Bute Hall valued highly: grammatically correct, perfectly spelt, filled with a wide variety of information – and mind-crunchingly dull. Just how had she managed to pull it off? She wasn't even sure she'd ever been to Dorset! And she had never in her life written anything without a single joke, cliffhanger or colourful metaphor. It was a truly remarkable achievement.

'All right girls,' said Miss Pretty, as she headed for the door. 'Finish up now; I'll be back in a moment; please make sure you've put your name at the top, then put your work on my desk.'

Rorie picked up her pen again, and was poised to write her name when Caroline appeared at her side. 'Careful!' she warned. 'Don't get ink on my sh—' As Rorie looked up, Caroline stopped dead in the middle of her sentence, her face turning white. 'What's happened to you?' she demanded.

'What's *happened* to me?' replied Rorie, touching her face. Was there some kind of weird delayed-effect from the lightning strike? She felt her face colour; was she going to have to own up about the whole incident? She attempted a casual laugh. 'What do you mean?'

Now a group of other girls began to huddle around. 'What happened to your hair?' said one. 'And where did those freckles come from?' asked another.

Rorie took the end of her ponytail and tried to inspect it: it *did* seem to be lighter than usual, but this couldn't have happened as a result of the lightning strike – could it? 'I...freckles?' Rorie did not have one single freckle normally.

'Aaargh!' cried Caroline suddenly. She was staring at the pages of writing on Rorie's desk. She picked them up. 'That's my handwriting!' she exclaimed.

Everyone gasped.

Now Caroline's expression turned to one of grave suspicion. 'Just what are you up to?' she demanded.

So many thoughts were crowding Rorie's mind at this moment, she didn't know what to say or do. She blinked up at Caroline's pale-skinned face, with its mass of freckles, framed by light-brown hair... no!

This was freaky...

She stood up. 'I...I'm not *"up to"* anything!' she insisted, trying to get the pages back. 'Now leave me alone.'

But Caroline snatched the pages away from her. '"Grandparents in Dorset...stables...two-year-old bay",' she read. 'This is all about *my* half-term! How dare you!'

The others gasped again, and began muttering among themselves. Rorie was mortified...and scared. What was going on? She reached again for the pages, ripped them from Caroline's hands and ran for the door. Just as she was leaving, she bumped into Miss Pretty as she was returning to the class.

'Where are you going?' asked the teacher.

'I...don't feel well!' shrieked Rorie, and she bolted down the corridor before Miss Pretty could say another word, clutching the ripped pages tightly.

Panting deeply, she slammed the door to the toilets and ran over to the mirror. 'Aaah!' she cried, clamping her hands to her cheeks. She did look different – and more than a little bit like Caroline. Caroline's face, Caroline's handwriting, Caroline's memories...Caroline's *shirt*.

Chapter 16
Chameleon Girl

Rorie tugged impatiently at her cravat. 'Oh, get off!' she grunted loudly as she yanked it off, then the tunic, and finally the shirt, which she threw to the ground as if it were red hot. *Now...*now she would see...

She stared at her reflection. *Oh please, please go back to normal!* Someone was bound to come along any moment. She wondered what they were all saying about her right now, back in the classroom. How was she going to explain this? What would they all think of her now? She peered closer, turning her face to left and right. She undid her ponytail to get a better look at her hair. She stared at her nose, where most of the freckles were. It made her go cross-eyed, but she did her best to count them. ...Seven, eight, nine, ten...

Hang on. That one right on the bridge of her nose...there *had* been one there, hadn't there? Start again: one, two, three, four…aha! She caught one mid-fade, watched in awe as it disappeared from her face. Yes! Now they were going more rapidly…and her hair! Her hair really was getting darker.

Someone was coming; Rorie quickly gathered up her things, dived into the nearest cubicle and locked the door.

'Rorie?' came Caroline's voice, loud with rage. 'I know you're in there, and I want my shirt back!'

Rorie said nothing, just flipped the shirt over the top of the cubicle door. She watched as it was snatched away.

'Thanks…*weirdo*.'

'You're *welcome* to it,' retorted Rorie with all the hostility she could muster.

The door swung shut, and Caroline was gone.

Rorie ripped the essay into tiny pieces, and flushed them down the toilet. As she watched them disappear, images flashed before her eyes: her hand grabbing that umbrella shaft; the lightning bolt; Arthur Clarkson's little bundled-up body tumbling forth as Elsie prayed, 'unto the Father, and unto the Son, and into the hole he goes…'

Silly Elsie! Rorie had said. 'It's "*unto the Holy Ghost.*"'

And in memory of the Ghost of Arthur Clarkson, here was Rorie Silk: Chameleon Girl.

'Oh, my dear girl,' said Pat, 'whatever's the matter; did you take a turn for the worse?'

Rorie massaged her forehead. 'Yes. I have a headache.' Now completely restored to her normal appearance, she had changed back into her own clothes and dashed over to sickbay. 'I thought I was better, but...I think I need to lie down.'

'Oh, love, come here, rest yerself,' gushed Pat. 'D'you want me to call the doctor?'

'No,' said Rorie, 'I think I just wasn't quite ready to go back to school,' she lied.

'All right,' said Pat, shaking out a couple of aspirins. 'I'll tell Mr Silk you need a little more time to convalesce...and just let him breathe one word about malingering, and I'll give him such a piece of my mind, he won't know what's hit him!'

'Thanks, Pat,' said Rorie, as she took the tablets and washed them down with water. The nurse might be an old soak, she mused, but her heart was in the right place – which was more than could be said for Uncle Harris or Aunt Irmine. All the same, she mustn't know the truth about what had just happened, if it could be helped.

Pat's Shel beeped; she consulted it and sighed. 'Oh, another sports injury. I always tell them that game's too violent, but nobody listens to me.' She took a swig from her mug, then picked up her first aid kit and headed for the door. 'You just rest up for a while, dear. Bye for now.'

Thank heaven for hammerball, thought Rorie. She was still reeling in shock, and would have gone half out of her mind if she'd had to make small talk with Pat, when all she really wanted to do was turn things over in her mind and see if she could make any sense of them. For one thing, how much did Miss Pretty know? Caroline would have told her all about what had happened, Rorie was sure of that. But as far as the essay was concerned, all Caroline had was just a few tiny scraps with random words on them. Not enough to convince anyone that this was anything more than a routine squabble. Then there was Rorie's appearance; how much would Miss Pretty have been able to see? But Rorie had been careful not to look directly at Miss Pretty when she had been dashing out of the class. Added to that, the corridor was dingy, and Rorie's collar had half-concealed her face. Given that this was also the first time they had ever met, Rorie didn't think Miss Pretty would have noticed whether her appearance had changed – or even that she'd notice next time she saw her.

Having satisfied herself on that point, Rorie turned her thoughts to the bigger picture: just what had happened, and what did it all mean? If what she was thinking was true – that somehow she had absorbed chameleon-like qualities from Arthur Clarkson when they had been shot through with that lightning bolt – then the possibilities were mind-blowing. Eyeing a cardigan Pat had left behind, slung over the back of a chair, she took a deep breath and braced herself; she would have to test the theory.

She put the cardigan on, went over to the mirrored cabinet and watched. She stared so hard, her reflection began to swim in front of her and she had to look away. Now she felt incredibly nervous; the idea of turning into a rather overweight middle-aged woman repulsed her. But she had to know, and right now. She tried to turn back to the mirror, then lost her nerve. So instead of studying her reflection, she looked down at her body.

And it was changing.

She was filling out her T-shirt like never before; two great mounds were forming on her formerly scrawny chest, straining against the fabric. In fact, her whole middle section seemed to be puffing up like a balloon, and now she could no longer see her feet. She felt like Alice after eating the slice of cake marked 'EAT ME'...oh, this was just too weird! Part of her just wanted to throw off the cardigan – yet she forced herself not to, hugging it to her instead. She knew her face was changing too, but couldn't bring herself to look. Instead, she put her hand up and felt around; sure enough, her own taut, smooth skin had developed an unpleasant sponginess.

Breathe, Rorie told herself. *Stay calm.* She knew she only had to take off the cardigan to go back to normal. But this was only part of the transformation; she had to keep the cardigan on long enough to see if she developed any of Pat's...what? Nursing skills? How was she going to test that? She hadn't thought this through. She glanced around the room, hoping that something would occur to her. Suddenly a strange urge consumed her and she found herself reaching into the small fridge nearby, grabbing the milk carton and pouring its contents into the mug Pat had left out on the table. What came out wasn't milk...but Rorie wasn't surprised; she had expected this. What was more, she wanted to drink it.

Enough! Rorie tore off the cardigan, and the sickly urge immediately began to fade.

It was past dinnertime and Pat, having decided to keep Rorie company for a while, was well-sauced. Meanwhile, Rorie had been doing some thinking.

'Do Uncle Harris and Aunt Irmine go out much?' she asked Pat.

'Pah! Hardly ever,' said Pat. 'Dull as ditchwater...sorry, *hic*! Shouldn't say that...blood relatives and all that...'

'No, it's OK,' said Rorie.

'Just the usual Sunday lunch thing down in the village...same every week, reg'lar as clockwork, hic! 'Zact same time, same place, same table, same meal...right down t' the number o' peas on the blasted plate, shouldn't wonder...thass 'bout it. More 'sitement down the bleedin' morgue, I reckon...sorry, *hic*!'

'No really, it's OK,' insisted Rorie. This was good; the more drunk Pat got, the less guarded she was about "opening her big mouth and putting her foot in it"...and the more likely she was to forget she'd ever said anything in the first place. 'That's it? They never go anywhere any other time?'

'Not unless there's a funeral...or that Annual Head Teacher's thingy.'

And we've only just had that, thought Rorie: *good*. She watched as Pat's eyelids began to droop... 'So, they don't really go out much...at *night*?' she asked, trying to make it sound like an idle enquiry.

'She might go ter her sisster now 'n' then,' yawned Pat. 'But other than that, nah.'

'I suppose they mainly need two cars for, uh, errands and stuff, then,' remarked Rorie nonchalantly. She'd noticed another car parked alongside Uncle Harris's, and needed to be sure it belonged to Aunt Irmine.

'Errands an' stuff, yeah...' said Pat vaguely, then opened one eye wide and stared at Rorie. 'Hey, why the twenty questions?'

'Oh, nothing, just curious,' said Rorie averting her gaze. 'So, uh, Aunt Irmine sometimes goes off by herself, then?'

Pat sighed; she was drifting. 'Yeah...' Then she sprawled herself sideways across the table and within moments was snoring.

She stirred briefly when, a few minutes later, Elsie was brought in by Leesa Simms. 'Oh! Hello there!' she said cheerily, momentarily transforming into her bright and breezy sober morning self, before promptly falling right back to sleep the moment Leesa had gone.

'What happened?' asked Elsie.

Rorie jumped up and closed the door. 'You're not going to believe it! And I think I've got a plan for our escape.'

Chapter 17
Witch Hunt

By the next morning, Rorie realised she could fake illness no longer. Besides, being around Pat Dry was getting her down. Quite apart from the drunkenness, Rorie found the constant reminder of what it felt like to 'be' Pat, even for those few minutes, quite nauseating.

All the same, she didn't relish the prospect of facing Caroline, Joyce and the rest of them one little bit. At least Alison Clingfilm was back; Rorie had never been so pleased to see her. She might be intensely annoying, but at least she was friendly. 'Hey,' said Rorie, as she finished bundling up her things for the laundry. 'How are you doing?'

'Oh…hi,' said Alison vaguely, seemingly intent on finding something in her locker.

Rorie frowned. 'Is something the matter?'

Alison said nothing, just glanced nervously at Joyce, who was hovering nearby, before diving further into her locker.

Joyce brushed past Rorie. 'Witch,' she whispered, then moved on.

Rorie whirled around. '*What* did you say?' she demanded.

Joyce smirked at her. 'You heard.'

Rorie snapped. 'Oh, don't be so ridiculous! I'll—' she was about to say she'd report her for bullying, but who would she report to? And what would her explanation be?

'Yes?' said Joyce, hand on hip.

Rorie turned to Alison. 'What have they been saying about me?'

'Nobody's said anything, Rorie,' insisted Alison, though she still wouldn't look her in the eye. 'I don't know what you're talking about.'

'Oh come on; didn't you hear her just now? She called me a witch...Alison!'

But Alison had turned around and was heading out of the room. Most of the others were doing the same; some looked back at Rorie from a safe distance, whispering to each other. Rorie pictured herself burning at the stake, and right now she was burning up inside. Alison may have been annoying before, but at least Rorie counted her as an ally – and now she had turned her back on her. How could she!

'Are you surprised?' said Joyce. 'She doesn't want you casting spells on her, and neither do the rest of us. So just back off, OK? Oh, and by the way; Nikki Deeds knows about this.' Then she turned on her heel and left.

And so it continued for the rest of the day. When Rorie was queueing for lunch with her tray, it momentarily came into contact with the one belonging to the girl in front of her. The girl turned around. 'Back off, *Devil's child*!' she hissed, clutching her tray to her chest and squeezing up next to the girl in front of her.

Rorie ate her lunch surrounded by a vast empty space. *Fine*, she thought. *I don't like you lot either*.

At least it meant that when Elsie came over to join her, they had some privacy. 'Why you on your own?' asked Elsie.

'Huh, why do you think?' said Rorie. 'I'm either a witch or the Devil's child – not sure which. Hah! Which witch. Hey, maybe I'm both...*can* you be both?'

'You should of said how come you can change like

that,' said Elsie.

Rorie rolled her eyes. 'Oh, *right*. "Hey guys, nothing to worry about. I was just struck by lightning while holding a chameleon, and now I've absorbed some chameleon-like qualities. That's all!"'

'Well!' said Elsie indignantly. 'Surely it's better than being a witch or a devil! I think it's *brilliant*; I wish I could do it. You're lucky!' Elsie had been sorely disappointed the previous evening when Rorie had refused to put on Pat Dry's cardigan again for her benefit.

Lucky: Rorie hadn't had a chance to consider it in this light yet. 'Well, I guess that's one way of looking at it. But right now I don't *feel* lucky. It hurts. This lot would never even try to understand such a thing, don't you see? Probably the only person who would is Moll, and she's not here; besides her, the only "friend" I had is too much of a wimp even to get my side of the story. Not that that would help anyway...oh, I can't wait to get out of here!'

'Let's do it today then!' said Elsie.

'No, it's OK. Besides, I've been thinking some more; those Perfects have some very useful skills, you know. It would be a waste not to do something about that.'

'Like what?'

'Like get hold of a piece of clothing!' explained Rorie, lowering her voice further still, even though the noise of the canteen combined with the distance from everyone else provided a virtually cast-iron certainty that nobody could hear a word. 'But it would have to be something small; socks, for example – or a cravat. Think you can manage that?'

'Me?'

'It *has* to be you, Else; I'm the Devil, remember? Things are bad enough for me right now.'

'But look what happened when I went looking for dress-up stuff,' Elsie pointed out.

'Just try not to get caught,' said Rorie. 'Oh go on; what can they do to you, anyway? Just have a go...please? Just think what I'd be able to do in Nikki Deeds' socks!'

'Ooh, I see what you mean,' said Elsie, excited now. 'I seen her, she does the highest jump of anybody.'

'Exactly!' said Rorie. 'And Leesa Simms' cravat. If what you tell me about her computer skills is true, then who knows? That could come in handy too at some point. Do it please, Else?'

'Please Miss, I need the loo,' said Elsie, her hand shooting up during that afternoon's Maths lesson.

Through the window she had just spotted both Perfects and their class, marching military style towards the field in their P.E. kit, their hammers resting on their shoulders.

'The "loo"?' said Aunt Irmine disparagingly. 'And what is the "loo"?'

'Sorry,' said Elsie. 'I mean the toilet.'

'No visits to the bathroom during lessons, Elsa; you know the rules.'

Elsie squirmed. 'But Miss, *please*...I fink I got the squits!' She crossed her legs and pulled the most desperate face possible.

'The...what?' said Aunt Irmine, intent on making her suffer.

Elsie squirmed some more. What was the proper word? 'I mean – you know, the runs...' There was much stifled giggling in class. 'Um...I got a dire rear—'

'Oh go along,' said Aunt Irmine at last, shooing her away.

Elsie limped out of the room, to more chuckles. 'Quiet now, please,' said Aunt Irmine. Everyone immediately fell silent, like the little angels they all were.

Elsie, now more familiar with the school's layout, raced along the labyrinth of corridors. Twice she was stopped by teachers, and twice she lied, saying she'd been sent to fetch something. She knew the cameras would tell a different story, but she didn't care any more; besides, she would dream up some elaborate explanation if she had to.

The changing rooms were in an ancient draughty annex, all icy flagstone floors and iron hooks. Pristine rows of neatly labelled kit bags hung from the hooks, and perfectly polished shoes were lined up in little cubby holes. 'A place for everything, and everything in its place,' Elsie remembered Aunt Irmine saying. At least it made the bags easy to identify; in no time at all, Elsie had found the one belonging to Leesa Simms. Carefully following her sister's instructions, she took out the cravat and swapped it for her own, so as not to arouse suspicion. She even peeled off Leesa's nametape and tried to stick it to the other cravat; it wouldn't stick properly, but it would have to do. Elsie stuffed her own cravat into Leesa's bag and moved on to Nikki Deeds' hook. Elsie pulled from her pocket the pair of Rorie's socks she had given her to swap, since her own would be too small. But she could find no socks in Nikki's kitbag. There *was* a cravat – but somehow this didn't seem as if it would have the desired effect.

Then Elsie spotted the laundry hamper – just as breathless chatter and running footsteps signalled the approach of some girls. Desperate, Elsie began throwing items out of the hamper. Then – bingo! –she spotted a soft, washable training shoe. Inside was a label bearing the name 'Nikki Deeds'.

Chapter 18

Against the Rules

Rorie couldn't remember the last time she had been so pleased to see someone. She had left the refectory early to do some research in the nearest computer room, and as she was leaving she saw Moll wheeling her case in through the hall. She was in mufti; although Rorie had never seen Moll in her own clothes, they weren't what she had expected. She had on crisp, high-waisted trousers and a round-necked sweater, and her hair was tied in a ponytail.

Rorie ran up to her; 'Moll! You're back! How was the stupid Anger Management course?'

Moll smiled breezily. 'Oh, it wasn't stupid! How are you, Rorie?'

'Fine!' Rorie replied automatically. 'I mean, well no, actually,' she corrected herself as they walked down the hall. 'Things are pretty horrendous.'

'Oh, that's too bad,' said Moll.

Rorie stared at her, waiting for her to say something more, like, "Joyce been giving you a hard time?" or something. Nothing. Even the, "Oh, that's too bad" sounded hollow, completely devoid of sympathy.

'Yeah,' said Rorie. 'Well. How are you? Horrible to be back, eh?'

Moll paused, her head on one side. 'Do you know what? I missed this place! It's amazing how a bit of time away can change the way you feel about things. Do you ever find that?'

Now Rorie could barely believe what she was hearing. 'Right!' she laughed nervously. 'I'd miss this place like I'd miss having nails hammered into my head!'

Moll's polite smile was tainted with confusion. 'Ha ha! I...don't quite understand. Having nails hammered into your head would be *awful*!'

Rorie stopped in her tracks and put her hands on Moll's shoulders. 'Moll, what's happened to you? You've changed!'

'Change is part of growing up, Rorie; why are you surprised?'

Rorie was about to answer when Miss Pretty approached them, followed by Caroline Grey. 'Ah

Molly, glad to see you're back; go on up to your dorm and unpack your things.'

'Yes, Miss Pretty.'

'Rorie? You're to come with me and Caroline to the Head's office.'

Rorie had been expecting this. It was what she had been preparing for in the computer room: her defence over the Caroline's Shirt Incident. But she was so floored by her encounter with Moll, everything just flew out of her head and now she didn't have a clue what she was going to say.

How could Moll have changed so much? As she trailed behind Miss Pretty, Rorie examined everything Moll had said, struggling to find signs of the person she thought she knew, but it was no use: it was as if she were a different person.

Arriving at the doors of the Head Teacher's office, Rorie took a deep breath. *Stop thinking about Moll,* she told herself. *Concentrate on this*! One thing she was sure of: absolutely nobody must know about her secret. It was the key to her escape – and possibly a whole lot more. And after today's experiences, she was more determined than ever to escape.

Miss Pretty rapped on the heavy oak doors.

'Enter,' came Uncle Harris's stern voice from inside:

they entered. 'Ah, girls; sit down.' He seemed uneasy, regarding Rorie with the air of a squeamish boy poking at a slug with a stick. 'Now, Aurora, perhaps you'll tell me in your own words what happened in yesterday's I.S. lesson, hmm?'

Rorie stared at the picture on Uncle Harris's orderly desk, of Aunt Irmine from their wedding day; younger, darker-haired, wearing a meringue...and just as bulldog-like as ever. *What do I say?* Rorie asked herself, now gazing at an oddly fascinating lump of Perspex; some sort of paperweight, she supposed, or a puzzle.

'Well?'

OK, one thing at a time, Rorie told herself; *don't try to remember it all at once.* 'All right, I cheated,' she said at last. She turned to Caroline: 'I'm sorry.'

Caroline looked distinctly unimpressed.

'I did it because I was here in sickbay all half term,' Rorie explained to Uncle Harris, 'and I really didn't feel like writing about that. So instead I just put some stuff from a conversation I'd overheard that morning. It was a silly thing to do, and I won't do it again, I promise.'

Caroline scoffed.

'I see,' said Uncle Harris. 'And this stuff that you

heard was about Caroline Grey's half term, is that correct?'

'Yes.'

'Sir, she couldn't possibly have—' Caroline interrupted.

'Thank you, Caroline, we'll hear from you in a moment,' said Uncle Harris. He turned back to Rorie. 'And is it true that you had borrowed Caroline's shirt that day?'

Rorie shrugged. 'Yes.'

Uncle Harris and Miss Pretty exchanged glances. 'Well then: according to Caroline here, your, um...*appearance* altered as well. How do you explain that?'

Here was the tricky part. 'I can't,' admitted Rorie. 'Because it isn't true.' There: she'd said it.

Caroline gasped in disbelief. 'Are you calling me a liar?'

Her word against mine, Rorie reminded herself. 'No,' she said. 'M-maybe it was a trick of the light or something—' She was stalling, she knew it...she needed time to figure it all out...

'Oh *right*,' said Caroline sarcastically. She turned back to Uncle Harris. 'It's *witchcraft*, sir – I swear, I know what I saw! Besides, there was far more detail in what she wrote than she could possibly have known about.'

All three of them stared at her: Caroline, with her sneery, upturned freckled nose; Uncle Harris, with his knuckle face and weasel eyes; ugly Miss Pretty, with that sinister, squinty stare...

Rorie cleared her throat. Panic rose in her again, and her head began to throb... "Having nails hammered into your head would be *awful*!" said the voice of Moll-not-Moll – *no, don't think about that*! Rorie told herself. She stared at her hands, still marked in the palm by the lightning strike...memory loss...*am I losing my mind*?

No – that was it – the witchcraft! Caroline had said exactly what Rorie had wanted her to say. She stood up. 'Uncle Harris, I know what I did was wrong,' she announced. 'But I've said I'm sorry. Besides, what Caroline's saying doesn't even make sense; if I was a witch, why would I cast a spell on *myself*?' She glared at Caroline, newly confident, challenging her.

Caroline put her hands on her hips. 'Well—'

'*Also*,' Rorie interrupted, her blood pulsing through her veins. *Yes*! It was all coming together clearly in her mind now. 'I did a search of the digital Poker Bute Hall School Rule Book, and it's official:

witchcraft doesn't exist. It says so: page...uh, fif-fifty-two, clause 293...' She shut her eyes tightly, picturing the words: '"discussion of supernatural or occult matters is strictly forbidden, *since we do not recognise that such things exist.*"' She let out a deep breath as she opened her eyes.

The three Poker faces looked suitably taken aback. Even Uncle Harris raised an eyebrow as he surreptitiously consulted his computer. Rorie felt a glow of satisfaction; unsurprisingly, it looked as if this rule hadn't needed enforcing until now.

Caroline leapt to her feet. 'All right,' she announced defiantly, removing the kit bag from her shoulder. 'Just you watch; I can prove it!' She removed a shirt from the kit bag and handed it to Rorie. 'Go on! Try it on, Rorie.'

Rorie had feared this might happen, but she had been so busy remembering her rulebook quote, she'd neglected to think up a strategy. She looked at the shirt. 'Of course,' she said, taking it in what she hoped was a cool manner. As she slowly slid her arm into the sleeve, her mind ran through all the possible ways in which she might cause some kind of distraction. She would *have to*; there was no way she wouldn't soon start to look like Caroline...but all her ideas were of the 'oh look at that bird out there' sort...hopeless! Meanwhile, all eyes were on her as she now put her other arm into its sleeve. Caroline regarded her with beady-eyed concentration, already folding her arms in an attitude of triumph. If Rorie didn't come up with something soon, her precious secret would be out and all would be lost...

Suddenly, the room filled with the deafening ring of an alarm bell. Uncle Harris leapt to his feet. 'The fire alarm! We'll sort this out later...everybody outside, quick!'

Rorie couldn't believe her luck; as they headed towards the door, she removed the shirt and handed it back to Caroline.

'Just because we're going outside, doesn't mean you have to give it back,' remarked Caroline indignantly.

'Caroline, there's a *fire*,' retorted Rorie. 'Can you possibly think about something else for once?'

Soon the entire school was assembled outside, and everyone waited while the buildings were searched. People began to form small groups, chatting.

'Psst!' Rorie turned around and saw Elsie underneath the ancient cedar tree, beckoning to her; she hurried over.

'There's no fire,' whispered Elsie, grinning

mischievously.

Rorie gasped. 'You...?'

Elsie nodded. 'I was coming back from the changing room, an' I saw you 'fru Uncle Harris's window, an' I saw the girl giving you that shirt...'

Rorie took her sister's head in her hands and planted a kiss on her forehead. 'Oh, Elsie, you're brilliant! OK, did you get the things?'

'Well, I—'

But Elsie didn't have a chance to answer, as at that moment Aunt Irmine barrelled over to them, and ushered them back indoors.

Chapter 19
The Perfect Trainers

To Rorie's relief, there was no mention of returning to Uncle Harris's office after the fire drill; she guessed he felt that enough time had been lost, and everyone needed to get on with some work. She was off the hook for now...but she would have to dream up something clever for next time.

Then, after dinner that evening, Uncle Harris approached Rorie as she was about to leave the refectory. The moment she saw Elsie beside him, her heart skipped a beat. 'Is it...?'

'Your parents? No,' said Uncle Harris. 'We're relocating you within the school.'

Rorie felt disappointed and relieved at the same time: relieved, because she wasn't going for a re-play of the morning's exercise with Caroline's shirt.

'You two seem incapable of being anything but

trouble,' said Uncle Harris as they headed down the corridor, 'So we're just going to have to house you separately from the rest of the girls. Lessons will be conveyed via interactive screens and meals will be brought to you. Walk properly, child!' he reprimanded Elsie, who appeared to be limping slightly. 'You'll be escorted outside for exercise.'

'What, like in prison, you mean?' said Elsie.

Rorie nudged her; she was beginning to like this idea.

Uncle Harris's eyes flashed. 'Don't be absurd, you ungrateful child!'

The Friesan Wing was closed off for building works that had yet to start, and had doorways with yellow tape across them and signs saying, "DANGER! Unsound."

'What's an *un*sound?' whispered Elsie as they approached it, 'Does it mean the same as "silence"?'

'It's, uh, an adjective,' explained Rorie nervously. 'It means "unsafe"...um, Uncle Harris?'

'Your suite is at the other end,' explained Uncle Harris brusquely. 'It's quite safe.'

'I get a sweet?'

'It's like an apartment,' said Rorie, nudging her.

'Oh. Are there any sweets there?'

'No!' snapped Uncle Harris.

At the end of the corridor was a door. Uncle Harris punched out a code on the keypad, and the door opened onto a steep, winding staircase. At the top of the stairs was another door; he took out a big old-fashioned key, which made a loud grinding noise in the lock. They went in. The room had a high ceiling with exposed beams; it was furnished in nineteenth-century style, complete with four-poster bed, oil paintings and heavy velvet curtains. The only modern things were two wall-mounted screens.

'This was a former head teacher's quarters,' explained Uncle Harris. 'Not exactly like prison, hmm, Elsa?'

'Cor, I never seen a bed like that before!' gasped Elsie.

'You will see that all your things have been placed in the drawers,' said Uncle Harris. He picked up a remote control. 'You can access the entire school information circuit via the screens,' he said, demonstrating with the remote, 'and there are headphones for your lessons. Any questions? Good.' And before the girls had the chance even to formulate any questions in their heads, let alone ask them, he was gone.

Elsie didn't care. 'Whee!' she went, throwing herself onto the bed.

'Ssh!' said Rorie, hearing a grinding noise. She ran to the door and tried to open it. 'He's locked us in!'

'Oh,' said Elsie, gazing blankly at the door.

Rorie was stunned. 'Wow. This really *is* like a prison!'

'But one with a bouncy bed!' added Elsie cheerfully, jumping up and down once more. 'Aargh!' she cried a split-second later, when the mattress caved in at the middle, almost swallowing her up.

'Oh Elsie!' sighed Rorie, running over. She climbed up onto the bed and helped her out of the pit. 'Good grief, this bed must be decades old!' She pulled back the covers to reveal an ancient sprung mattress with half the springs gone. 'Eurgh! And the bedspread's all moth-eaten. This place has been empty for years...oh my God, this is worse than ever; how are we going to escape now, Else?'

Elsie hung her head. 'I dunno...oh!' She began crying. 'I want Mummy and Daddy!'

Rorie put her arm around her, and a lump rose in her throat. 'I know...and this police investigation is taking *forever*.'

'They don't care!' wailed Elsie.

Rorie brushed a tear from her own cheek and sniffed. 'No, that's not true; they *do* care,' she said, as she began changing into her slants. 'Just not in the way that we do...how could they? It's not their own mum and dad...' She went to the window. 'Oh, we so need to get out of here!' The window opened easily; Rorie stuck her head out.

Elsie joined her. 'Can we jump?'

Rorie sighed, pulling herself back in. 'No, it's way too high.'

'Well I got you some things,' said Elsie.

'Oh, great!' said Rorie, watching as Elsie delved into the deep pocket of her oversized tunic and pulled out the cravat and one soft, super-light trainer.

Rorie's face fell. 'That's it?'

'Well, I couldn't get the socks.'

Rorie inspected the label on the shoe. 'OK, it's Nikki's, but...*one shoe*? What am I supposed to do with that?' Her heart sank as an image formed in her head of a half-Rorie, half Nikki figure, split down the middle.

'Hang *on*,' said Elsie, now fumbling under her skirt. 'My other pocket's got a hole...oh, it's stuck.' She pulled up her skirt and there, its laces knotted around her leg, was the other trainer.

'Oh, fantastic!' gasped Rorie, down on her knees now and eagerly untying it. Elsie, you're a star! I knew this ghastly uniform had to be good for something.'

'I just knotted it lotsa times, 'cause I couldn't do rabbit ears,' explained Elsie.

'I can't believe you've been walking around like this...there!' Rorie clutched the trainers to her chest. It was almost as if a prayer had been answered; she remembered how she had been mesmerised by the flying goddess Nikki Deeds as she watched her doing the high jump, and wished she could trade places with her. Now she could actually *be* that flying goddess – temporarily, at least. Rorie felt a tingle of excitement; finally, some good might come of this whole chameleon thing! The only problem was, she might never want to take the trainers off...

'Eew, what's that smell?' she said, sniffing. 'Eurgh, it's the trainers! Who'd have thought the flying goddess could have such smelly feet?' She leaned out of the window again. 'It's a long way down, even for a Nikki-Deeds-style jump...' She pulled herself back in and looked at the bed. 'The sheets: if I could get part of the way down, maybe I could jump the rest of the way. Then I can come back for you.'

'But the door'll be locked,' Elsie pointed out.

Rorie slapped her head. 'Oh! Of course, what am I thinking…a ladder; that's what we'll need.'

'Luke would have one,' said Elsie.

Rorie clicked her fingers. 'Right. We need to figure out where his shed is from here…I know, the school network.' She picked up the remote and flicked a screen to life. 'What wing did Uncle Harris say we were in?'

'The Freezing Wing, I fink.'

'He's not kidding,' said Rorie, shivering as she navigated her way round the school website. 'Ah, this must be it: the *Friesan* Wing…and there's the Groundsman's Quarters; it's not far at all…Else? What is it?'

Elsie picked something small off the floor. 'Rorie, I've just had a *brilliant* idea!' she said, proudly presenting her with a dead moth. 'Wings! I stick this on your back, then you'll be like a moth and be able to fly!'

'Don't be ridiculous!' said Rorie, as she went about pulling the sheets off the bed. 'That wouldn't work!'

'How do you know if you don't try?' replied Elsie, following her around with the moth.

'I just *know*,' said Rorie, busily twisting the sheets. 'Get off me!'

'But you wear someone's shirt and you turn into them—'

'I do not!' said Rorie indignantly. 'I just…take on *aspects* of that person, that's all. I'm still me, Elsie.'

'OK, so you could take on *ass-bets* of the moth, right?'

Rorie rolled her eyes. 'It's not the same! Besides, it's dead.'

Elsie gazed forlornly at the moth. She had no idea whether that made a difference or not, but in any case she was suddenly horrified at the image of her sister as half-girl, half-moth. 'Oh well,' she sighed, tossing the moth away. 'A swan; that's what we need…' A half-Rorie, half-swan; now *that* was far more appealing. Perhaps she could even ride on her back! And if no swans were available, then…'Hey, what about feathers? From the pillows!'

'They're *synthetic*,' snapped Rorie, and that was an end to it. She finished changing into her own casual clothes, then picked up the smelly trainers: now for the moment of transformation. She put them on.

She felt her heart quicken, as she was overcome by a strange mix of panic, excitement and dread. Panic, because no matter how much she longed to have a go at being Nikki Deeds, the sense of losing oneself was still alarming; excitement, because she did so much want this experience all the same – and dread, because her plan might not work.

Elsie stood close to her, staring intently.

Rorie inched away. 'Don't do that!'

'What?'

'That *staring*. It won't make it happen any quicker, you know.'

'Sorry. Oh, hey...your hair's getting lighter!'

'Really?' Rorie walked over to the mirror. 'That's faster than last time.'

Her nose became smaller, her cheeks rounder; her shoulders grew broader. 'Wow!' she gasped, as she flexed her arm muscles. 'I feel *strong*.' She did a cartwheel across the floor, then a couple of back-flips, finishing in a perfect pose.

'Whoo-hoo, it really works!' cried Elsie. 'Hey, it's not fair; *I* want magic powers too!'

'It's not magic, silly. Its just—'

'What?' challenged Elsie. 'Looks like magic to me.'

'Hey, this feels goo-ood!' exclaimed Rorie, limbering up. 'Whoo! I feel sorry for people who aren't as perfect as me...oops!' She clapped her hand to her mouth. 'I can't believe it...why did I say that?'

'Because it's what Nikki Deeds would say?'

suggested Elsie.

'Really? I mean yes, I guess it must be, but…I didn't know she was like that. Huh.'

Elsie shrugged. 'It figures.'

Rorie remembered Joyce's boasts of being great pals with Nikki. 'I suppose so. It's so weird…I'm still me, but then something like that will slip out when I'm not looking. Anyway,' she said, finishing her stretches, 'lets get out of here.' She knotted the sheets together, tied one end to a crossbeam in the vaulted ceiling, then pulled the sheet-rope over to the window. It didn't go very far. 'Hmm,' she said, taking another look outside. 'I've got another idea.'

'Oh Rorie, I'm scared you're gonna fall!' said Elsie.

'Well…it *is* pretty dangerous,' admitted Rorie. 'But I've done this sort of thing loads of times before…I mean *Nikki* has. Trapeze work, that is. I'm going up, not down. I just swing out of the window, do a somersault, then swing my legs over the parapet. Then I jump down to the extension roof.'

'Oh, is that all!'

Rorie leapt onto the sheet and began swinging herself backwards and forwards, a little higher each time.

Creak, creak! went the knotted sheet on the beam.

Higher, higher...

...Now she was swinging right out of the window each time; this was what she had been waiting for. Three, two, one—

NOW!

Straining against the upper frame of the window, the sheet bent at an angle and launched Rorie straight upwards. Nikki Deeds' strategy was all there, a voice in her head telling her exactly when to let go...Rorie felt herself sailing through the air, rolling head over heels, a flying goddess...*Now flip your legs back*, said the voice, *and lock them over the parapet*...Yes! She was there.

Chapter 20
The Grey Jacket

'All right,' said Rorie, as they crept towards their uncle and aunt's cottage, shrouded in darkness. 'Now we have to steal something of Aunt Irmine's.'

'What?'

'They don't lock their place. I found out from Pat Dry when she was drunk. There's no need, you see, with a guard at the gate, and electric fences around the grounds.'

'But why—?'

'I'm going to drive us out of here in Aunt Irmine's car,' said Rorie. 'Trust me; I've figured it all out. Just follow my instructions…OK,' she whispered, as they drew near to the cottage. 'From now on, not a sound.' She managed to sound calm, but inside she was a jangle of nerves. The gymnastics had been scary enough, but coaxing a terrified Elsie down the tall, wobbly ladder – *wearing* Rorie's backpack – had been a nightmare. At least no one had been around to hear all the noise – their isolation had worked to their advantage. Not so here.

As it turned out, Uncle Harris and Aunt Irmine were making enough noise of their own; they were having an argument in the kitchen.

'...I just don't see why you can't try again,' came Aunt Irmine's voice, amplified by the shiny surfaces. Peering from behind a rosebush, Rorie watched as she moved briskly around the room, tidying up.

'I've said, I'm *going* to!' retorted Uncle Harris.

'Well, *when*?' shrieked Aunt Irmine, slamming a cupboard door. 'She's 112 years old, for heaven's sake! She could go at any time! We've got to get that will made over to you before it's too late.'

Rorie made a tiny gasp; so she had been right!

'Look, I'm working on her!' protested Uncle Harris. 'When she finally sees sense, I'll give Lister a call...Oh! If only those two brats had been in that car with their parents, we wouldn't have this problem.'

Aunt Irmine softened, united with her husband against the common enemy. She sighed. 'Oh, you're right there...if only!'

'They mean *us*?' gasped Elsie.

Roric clamped a hand to her mouth. 'Ssh!'

Uncle Harris left the room, as Aunt Irmine went about preparing some tea. Then she put mugs and biscuits onto a tray, and carried it out of the kitchen.

It was time.

Rorie took the backpack from Elsie. 'Go and ring the front door bell, then hide,' she whispered.

'OK!' nodded Elsie, springing into action.

'Hey – do it twice,' Rorie added hastily. 'But don't get caught!'

Rorie dashed for the back door. She waited for the muffled ring of the doorbell, *brr-rrr-rr-rrt*! then softly, softly turned the handle. It opened easily. She slipped out of the Nikki Deeds trainers, then realised to her dismay that her socks were now tainted with the same strong, cheesy smell. Ugh! She hurriedly removed them, then crept into the small kitchen.

She heard Aunt Irmine's voice at the front door: 'Hello? Who's there?'

Rorie peered around desperately; she had hoped to find a jacket hanging over a kitchen chair or something, but there was only a handbag. She slipped in her hand, took a 20 note from her aunt's wallet, and pocketed it. She heard the front door close, and Aunt Irmine muttering to herself. Rorie crouched behind the table.

'Who was it?' came the muffled voice of Uncle Harris.

'Nobody. Must be something wrong with our doorbell.'

Come on Elsie, ring again! thought Rorie.

Brr-rrr-rr-rrt! At last! There was the bell again.

'Oh, what in heaven's name…!' Aunt Irmine, irritated, turned back.

Close to the kitchen doorway, Rorie could see Aunt Irmine's grey jacket hanging on a coat rack. But it was *right there in the hall*, and Rorie was so nervous she felt as if she might just turn to liquid then and there, become nothing but a puddle on the floor. Still, it was now or never; she tiptoed over. Her heart leapt as she saw into the living room out of the corner of her eye, where Uncle Harris sat with his back to her.

'Hello?' Aunt Irmine called into the night air.

Steeling herself, Rorie grabbed the jacket, and bolted toward the back door, getting there just as she heard the front door close for the second time. Gingerly closing the door behind her, she grabbed the socks and shoes and ran, barefoot, back to the rosebush. She put the smelly socks back on, then carefully put the Nikki Deeds trainers in her backpack and took out her own shoes.

'Psst!' she called, as the shadowy figure of Elsie appeared.

Elsie trotted over. 'Did you get something?'

'Uh-huh,' nodded Rorie, holding up the jacket. She patted her sister on the back. 'Well done, Else. Come on.' She slipped on her shoes and backpack and led Elsie down the steeply terraced garden towards the carport, some twenty metres away from the cottage and shielded by trees.

Safely tucked behind one of these trees, Rorie sat down and composed herself. She was now plain Rorie again – but not for long. She put on the grey jacket. 'OK: now for Transformation Number Two...and no staring this time!' She turned her back to Elsie.

Elsie busied herself with pulling up tufts of grass.

'OK now, no screaming,' warned Rorie, after a few moments. 'I'm going to turn around.'

There was very little light, but enough for Elsie to see that Rorie had changed a good deal – for the worse. '*Eurgh*,' she gasped, with the same delighted revulsion as if she had stumbled upon a dead rodent.

'Mind your manners, young miss!' retorted Rorie-Irmine, as she got up and brushed herself down.

'No!' protested Elsie. 'Don't be like her!'

'Sorry,' whispered Rorie. She winced, repulsed by the jacket's unpleasantly familiar stale-perfume smell, and the bulldog-rugby-player-with-a-unibosom shape it had given her. 'Ugh, this gives me the creeps! But it's worth it, it's worth it...'

'Hey, does your fingerprint turn into Aunt Irmine's too?' asked Elsie.

'What, for the lock? No; same as the cottage; the car's probably not locked. Better not be, anyway; I don't change that completely...well, here goes.' She reached out and pulled the handle; *yes!* it opened.

'OK,' said Rorie, jumping into the driving seat, while Elsie got in the back. 'Let's hope I can start this thing.'

Despite the awfulness of her Aunt Irmine guise, Rorie now felt a little thrill at the prospect of actually driving a car. How many times as a youngster had she sat behind the steering wheel and made that *hummm, hummm* sound of a hydrogen engine? Now the fantasy would become a reality; she would know what to do, because Aunt Irmine knew. At least, she hoped so; she didn't dare contemplate what would happen if she didn't. She must apply herself to the task, and give it her full concentration.

She pressed the 'scan override' button; as with the

fingerprint, she knew that the scan for analysing the iris of the eye would not identify her as Aunt Irmine, and therefore not start the car. So she would have to start up the way any guest driver would; with the four-digit code. Having access to Aunt Irmine's knowledge, she was able to do just that. The number popped into her head: 6279. She tapped it in, and the car sprang to life, thrumming gently and turning on its lights. Rorie quickly turned them off, so as not to be seen.

Good evening, said the car. *Please state your destination.* The screen on the dash lit up.

Rorie was momentarily flustered, then blurted out, 'Butehurst...er, train station.'

Thank you, said the car, and the screen presented all the data for the journey; distance, estimated arrival time, road conditions.

'Now remember,' Rorie warned Elsie, as she released the emergency brake. 'Keep low.' The car eased down the driveway. Once they were well away from the cottage, Rorie put the headlights back on. Approaching the security gate, she felt a flutter of nerves. But, she reminded herself, what would the guard see? A familiar car, apparently driven by its usual driver. Off to visit her sister, as she sometimes did. It was dark, Rorie was wearing Aunt Irmine's jacket, and she looked at least somewhat like her. She briefly glanced at her reflection in the mirror: pudgy-faced, bulldog-jawed; thin, greying hair. She quickly looked away in digust; *that should do the job,* she reassured herself. After all, the guard wouldn't even suspect an imposter; he'd probably barely glance at her...unless they were in the habit of exchanging pleasantries. But then, Aunt Irmine exchanged pleasantries with no one.

And just as she expected, the guard just nodded at her and raised the barrier.

They were free.

Chapter 21
Embarrassing Costume

Rorie raced along the deserted country road at ninety kilometres per hour, ignoring the voice of Aunt Irmine in her head that was nagging her to 'Slow down! Slow down!'

'Yee-haa!' cried Rorie. 'We did it, Else; we did it!'

'Yee-hoo!' echoed Elsie, now strapped into the back seat. 'Hey, I want a go at drivin'.'

'No way,' shrieked Rorie. 'Are you crazy?'

''Snot fair,' said Elsie petulantly. 'You get all the fun.'

'Stop that this instant,' demanded Rorie, sounding like Aunt Irmine again.

Elsie fell silent, then asked, 'So what's it feel like?'

'What, driving?'

'Yeah.'

'It's cool,' said Rorie, downplaying it all she could.

It felt *fantastic*. 'But I am *not* enjoying "being" Aunt Irmine; count yourself lucky.' She slowed down, her mind filling with practical thoughts. 'We're going to have to abandon this car, you know.'

'What? We don't get to keep it?'

'Are you kidding? Look, for all we know, they might already have noticed the missing jacket, the car...they could be onto the police by now, and we'd be tracked down in this, no trouble. No: we dump it at the train station and...get on a train somewhere.'

Stopping alongside another vehicle at a traffic light on the outskirts of Butehurst, Rorie suddenly felt very conspicuous. Even though she knew she looked older, she couldn't shake the feeling that the other driver knew she was too young to drive – could possibly even read the guilt on her face. She stared straight ahead at the light, waiting for it to change...

Green light; the other car sped away.

In 200 metres, turn right, said the car.

Rorie followed the car's instructions to the station, moving effortlessly among the town's evening traffic. Roundabouts, pedestrian crossings, even other bad drivers didn't trouble her. Then she heard a police siren. Glancing in her rear-view mirror, she felt the panic rise as she saw the flashing blue light; it was coming nearer.

'You think they're after us?' asked Elsie.

'How the heck would I know?'

'Shouldn't we try an' get away, just in case?'

'No!' said Rorie. 'That's a sure-fire way of drawing attention to ourselves.' She didn't mention that she was very tempted to do just that. Instead, she did as the other drivers were doing; she pulled over to let the police through.

WEEYAWEEYAW! went the siren, louder and louder – and then *vroom*, the police car whizzed past them.

'Phew!' sighed Elsie.

Rorie took a deep breath and drove on. 'OK, now to get rid of this thing.'

She was still congratulating herself when she turned into the station car park, and the car announced smoothly, *you have arrived at your destination*.

Then Rorie discovered how terrible Aunt Irmine was at parking.

She turned into a space, then reversed to straighten up – and failed to look first, to see if the way was clear. It wasn't; she nearly collided with a white van, whose driver honked loudly. ''Ere, look where you're going, you stupid cow!' yelled the driver.

Rorie made a crude hand sign at him, then gasped in shock at what she had just done.

'That's rude!' giggled Elsie.

The white van man swore loudly at her, before swerving off aggressively, wheels kicking up grit.

Rorie felt her face burn. 'That wasn't me did that; that was Aunt Irmine!'

'No way!' chuckled Elsie. 'Aunt Irmine swears? Oh, that is so excellent!'

They got out of the car, leaving it jutting out at a diagonal. Rorie took Elsie's hand and, looking for all the world as if she were her mother, led her into the station.

Now she was in a public space, Rorie felt very self-conscious, like being at a fancy dress party in an embarrassing costume. But as one person after another walked past, barely noticing her, she began to feel more at ease. *I'm an adult, I'm an adult,* she kept reminding herself.

'We goin' home?' asked Elsie.

'Yes,' said Rorie, who had only just decided on the plan. 'Although...' She studied the large black timetable overhead. 'I've no idea how we get to Edenfield from here. And, uh...neither does Aunt Irmine.'

'We could ask someone,' suggested Elsie.

'No way!' Rorie frowned at the timetable. 'Ah, Ocksted; that's near Edenfield. Come on.'

At the ticket machine, Rorie fished out the 20 and touched the screen for two child fares – no; one adult, one child fare to Ocksted. 'Oh.'

'What?'

Rorie pocketed the cash again. 'Haven't got enough,' she said under her breath, while still maintaining what she hoped was a cool, calm exterior. 'We'll need the money for food.'

At that moment a large, rowdy group of youths, all tattooed skulls and techno boots, were approaching the barrier from the other side. Neoskins. The guard bristled.

Perfect! Rorie quickened her pace, bringing Elsie towards the opposite end of the line of barriers from the Neoskins. While the guard was preoccupied with the unwieldy mass, mostly fare-dodgers, she guided Elsie under the barrier, and followed her through.

Much to Rorie's relief, the only other people near them on the hovertrain were some excitable young women, who hadn't even noticed them.

'I'm *starvin*',' moaned Elsie, hugging her stomach.

'Well, maybe we can get something at the other end.'

'Uuurgh!' Elsie groaned melodramatically. She embarked on a protracted scowl at her sister.

Rorie turned away from her. 'Stop that.'

'You look horrid,' said Elsie petulantly. 'When you going to go back to being you?'

'Hey! You wouldn't be *here* now if it weren't for my...*you know what,*' growled Rorie, a deep frown-line forming between her wispy brows. 'Anyway, I need the disguise. Believe me, I'm not staying like this a minute longer than I have to.'

Forgetting her hunger, Elsie suddenly became animated. 'Hey! We're going home!'

'Yes,' Rorie replied soberly. She wasn't sure how she was going to feel about that. But she felt a powerful urge to go there, as if an invisible thread were drawing her in.

Elsie's eyes widened and she leaned forward. 'Hey! You can put on some clothes of Mum's, and find out what's happened to her and Dad!'

'Elsie, I don't think—'

'What? You wear someone's cloves and they tell you what to do, right?'

'Well, in a way, but—'

'So you put on Mum's fings an' she can tell you what to do, can't she?'

Rorie sighed. 'Look, we still don't know how this whole thing works. I mean, I'm not sure wearing something of Mum's would work the way you think it would.'

'Why not?'

'OK: I wear Aunt Irmine's jacket and I know how to drive because *she* knows how to drive...'

'Only not park...'

'...Only not park. But what I've noticed is, it's all about practical skills. It seems I only get to use that person's knowledge when I try to *do* something they can do. Like, right now?' – she lowered her voice instinctively – 'I have no idea whether Aunt Irmine knows we're gone, or not. It's not like calling the person up on their Shel, you know.'

'Well, we can at least try, can't we?' insisted Elsie.

Rorie shrugged. 'All right, it can't hurt. But we don't *know* it will work, Elsie,' she added hastily. 'We just don't know.'

The snack bar at Ocksted was about to close for the night when they arrived, but Rorie just managed to get the man to sell her two packets of Wasabi SnakiSoys and a large shrink-pack of lychee iced tea. That was the good news. The bad news was, they had just missed the last bus to Edenfield.

'We'll have to spend the night somewhere round here,' said Rorie wearily, as they stood, shivering, at the deserted bus stop. There was no rain, but a damp March night chill clung to them. Now that all the excitement of the escape was over, Rorie felt quite overwhelmingly tired, and her limbs ached from all the exertion. She even abandoned her packet of SnakiSoys halfway through, too tired to eat. 'That's it,' she said, taking off the Aunt Irmine jacket. 'I can't bear to wear this thing a moment longer. I think it's giving me arthritis.' She pulled out the only two sweaters they had in the backpack, the thinfat ones which thickened in cold weather, and she and Elsie put them on.

'OK, just give me a moment,' said Rorie, as she began to change back into herself. 'Oh, that feels so much better! Aa-a-ah!'

'It's *so* weird,' said Elsie, still transfixed by the process as Rorie's hair went from dry and stiff to full and glossy, and her body elongated from a lumpen mass to the tall slender figure she really was.

'It's a gazillion times weirder for me, I can tell you,' said Rorie, stretching. 'All right; let's go.'

It wasn't long before they came to a supermarket. 'Let's go round the back,' suggested Rorie. 'There might be boxes.'

There *were* boxes; dozens of them. Above the supermarket were some offices, and a fire escape. 'We'll have to get the boxes up there if we can manage it,' said Rorie.

'Why?'

'Two words: *rats* and *foxes*.'

'Eeeyew!' squealed Elsie.

'Right. We learnt about it in school once – in *real* school. About life on the streets. Apparently boxes can be surprisingly warm and cosy; it's the vermin you have to watch out for.'

Mustering all the strength left in her weary limbs, Rorie managed to drag both her own box and Elsie's up the fire escape. Finally, exhausted, the two sisters climbed into their little homes and fell asleep.

Chapter 22
Going Home

Rorie was being prodded. She saw Joyce jabbing at her with her hammer, taunting her: 'Tackle the witch! Tackle the witch!' And the three Carolines, and Alison...*witch, witch, witch!*

'Wake *up*, Rorie. I need the loo!' came Elsie's voice. Prod, prod.

Rorie awoke to find she was scrunched up in a tunnel, her head resting on her backpack. Her feet were numb; behind Elsie, at the end of the tunnel, was light grey sky. 'Oh...' she groaned. 'The supermarket...'

'I'm going to pee my pants if I don't get to a loo right now!' demanded Elsie.

'Oh, OK, come on, I'll find somewhere for you to go,' groaned Rorie. She clambered out stiffly; she ached even more now. Nothing suitable presented itself until, heading back to the bus stop, they passed a building site with a mobile toilet cubicle.

Relieved, Elsie's mood was transformed. 'Yippee!' she cried, as she skipped along the deserted street. 'We're going home! I'm so excited!'

'Yes, but Mum and Dad *aren't there*, remember?' said Rorie, as they arrived at the bus stop.

'Yeah, but we're gonna *find* 'em now!' announced Elsie confidently.

Rorie bit her lip. Elsie made it sound as if it were just a case of going home and looking in the wardrobe or something, like Great-Grandma had said. 'Oh, ha ha, there you were all the time!' She seemed blissfully unaware of how much more complicated it was than that; to her, just escaping from Poker Bute Hall was half the battle. But even though Rorie knew better, she found Elsie's optimism infectious and uplifting. She smiled at her. 'Yeah!' she said. 'We are!'

'Hey – what about your disguise?' asked Elsie.

Rorie thought about Aunt Irmine's jacket and winced. 'I can't face it right now – it's really early, anyway; there's hardly anyone around. I'll put it on later if I have to.'

They remained in good spirits for the whole journey home; the early morning sun was slanting through the windows, they were free...everything felt wonderful. *We* will *find Mum and Dad*, thought Rorie. *We'll do the detective work.* Quite how they would go about it, she didn't have much idea; but home – and Mum's closet – seemed the logical place to start.

But their happy mood soon dissolved when they reached home. The windows were boarded up. Barbed wire surrounded the property, and a police sign outside announced that it was protected with an alarm.

They couldn't even get near.

'Oh, why didn't I think of this?' cried Rorie. 'I should've *known*...'

Beside her, Elsie began to disintegrate. 'Oo-o-oh!' she wailed, choked with sobs.

Rorie put her arm around her. 'I'm sorry, Else...I'm really sorry.' She gazed in disbelief at the house. It was *their* house – most of their possessions were still inside – yet they were locked out, banished. And they couldn't possibly go to the police and ask to be let in. Mum's beat-up old car still stood on the gravel drive in front, murky-windowed. The inside was littered with used tissues, water bottles, sweet wrappers, apple cores and a half-naked doll of Elsie's. The effect was eerie, as if Mum had just parked the car a few moments ago.

Elsie peered wistfully at the doll. '*Zee-Zee...*'

Rorie pulled on the door handle, but it was locked.

A door slammed next door. Rorie pulled Elsie back towards the shrubbery, where they waited until Vijay, Maya's husband from next door, disappeared down the road. Rorie consulted her watch. 'Blimey, he's off to work – it's already seven o'clock.'

'Hey, maybe we could go back and stay with them!' suggested Elsie. 'Or go round Molly's house...'

'Elsie! Look, I know they're good friends and everything, but you can't expect them to just let us come and stay...they'd have to report us, and then we'd be right back where we started. No, we've got to get away from here without being seen.'

Elsie sniffed, and wiped away a tear. 'Where we gonna go then?'

'I don't know,' Rorie admitted. 'Come on, I'll buy us some breakfast somewhere. I can hardly think, I'm so starved. That place on the motorway – they'll be open.'

'You can't have hot chocolate *and* a chocolate muffin,' said Rorie, as they moved along the display counter. 'You need some real food.'

'I can and I'm gonna, so there,' retorted Elsie, putting the biggest chocolate muffin of all on her plate. 'You're not a grown-up, so stop a-tending.'

'I am *not* pretending!' replied Rorie indignantly, putting the muffin back.

'Are too.' Elsie picked it up again.

'Am not!'

'Are too.'

The muffin went back and forth, back and forth. The youth behind the counter stared at them. Rorie sighed and gave in. 'Look, Missy,' she growled as she moved the tray along. 'I may not be an adult, but I'm five years older than you, and since we don't have an adult with us, what I say goes from now on, OK?'

'No-kay,' said Elsie defiantly.

Now they were at the checkout, so Rorie just flashed her a furious look and paid.

They sat in silence while Elsie indulged in her choc-fest, and Rorie filled up on her egg and bacon sandwich and yogurt drink. The food was bad, but the place was perfect; not somewhere they were likely to be recognised – or even noticed.

'So,' said Elsie, finishing up. 'Where we gonna go?'

Rorie was about to say something stinging about how it suited Elsie very well to let her be in charge when it came to figuring things out, but when she saw the big chocolate clown-smile on her face, she found it impossible to be cross with her. 'Wipe your face, Else,' she sighed, handing her a napkin. 'OK, here's an idea: just before…you know what happened…Mum had a big a clear out. Do you remember? She dropped off some bags of clothes at that second-hand shop on the Saturday afternoon.'

'Oh yeah!' said Elsie, smearing the chocolate marks across her face with the napkin.

'Well, it's a long shot, but we could test your theory…I mean, I really don't know what else to do.'

Chapter 23
The Dance of the Shop Ladies

Estella's Emporium was a big barn of a space, crammed with redundant clothes seeking new owners. Rorie couldn't help but feel a small thrill at the sound of her favourite radio station, Smooch BB, flinging her back into a world she'd been cut off from for two and a half weeks.

The girls flipped through a rack of tops. 'This stuff is *old*?' asked Elsie. 'Looks new to me.'

'That's the whole point,' said Rorie. 'According to Mum, Estella's a ghastly snob, *hates* it if you call the stuff "second hand". Oh, I don't see anything here; let's go look through the trousers.'

They had spent two nervous hours waiting for the shop to open, skulking around unloved corners of the urban landscape – the empty bit of the multi-storey car park, behind the recycling depot – to avoid being seen.

Then Rorie had insisted they wait for another customer to go into Estella's Emporium – again, to avoid being noticed. She needn't have worried; Estella, a middle-aged woman with impossibly black hair, sat behind her desk, too preoccupied with her phone conversation to notice anyone else.

Rorie sighed. 'Weren't there some white trousers of Mum's? Maybe they've been sold already...'

Elsie was too busy admiring her reflection in the mirror, holding a sequin top up against herself.

'Elsie!' hissed Rorie.

At that moment a woman came clattering into the shop in some absurd platform shoes. She had multicoloured hair extensions and multiple accessories which jangled and tinkled as she went. 'Sorry I'm late, Stel; got caught in traffic.'

Estella, finished with her phone call, rushed over to her excitedly. 'Never mind that,' she said, meeting her in the middle of the shop floor. 'Guess. Who's. Coming. Any minute now, *loaded* with designer cast-offs.'

Rorie and Elsie peered between the legs of a pair of mannequins that screened them from view.

Miss Multi paused in the chewing of her gum. 'Who?'

'Only *Nolita Newbuck*!'

There was a brief pause, then an ear-splitting 'Aaaaargh!' as Estella and Miss Multi held onto each other's arms and danced in a circle, screeching delightedly.

'Nolita Newbuck?' whispered Elsie, her voice masked by the noise the women were making. '*The* Nolita Newbuck?'

'Sounds like it,' whispered Rorie.

The dance of the shop ladies ended. 'She's not coming *personally*?' asked Miss Multi.

'No, of course not,' said Estella. 'But she's sending a whole van-load around – and we can use her name! I'm going to design some special labels *right now*.'

'Oh fantastic,' said Miss Multi. 'Tell you wot, I'll make us some tea, yeah? I'm gasping, me. Nolita Newbuck! Woo-hoo-hoo!' And off she jangled to the back room, while Estella went to the computer to compose her labels.

In the quiet that followed, the voice of the radio newscaster came to the fore, and Rorie jumped when she heard him say...*Aurora and Elsa Silk*.

Elsie gave a sharp intake of breath; Rorie put her hand over her mouth and they listened, transfixed:

...*Their abductor apparently used a resident*

*teacher's car to drive them out of the school grounds.
The car was later found nearby, but the whereabouts
of the girls is still unknown. Aurora, or 'Rorie', as she
is known, is twelve years old, tall with dark hair; Elsa
is seven with light brown hair. Anyone with
information as to the whereabouts of the two girls are
asked to contact Zedforce.com...*

Rorie dared not move a muscle; she managed just
the tiniest tilt of her head, to check if the shop had a
surveillance camera: it did. Somehow, they would have
to leave without being seen.

Miss Multi reappeared with the tea. 'D'you know,'
she said as she clattered and clanked her way over to
Estella, near the front of the shop. 'I reckon she's just
about as much of a star as all them people she's
discovered, is Nolita. She's amazing. Ere, an' guess
wot?'

'Woss that?' muttered Estella, her eyes fixed on the
computer screen.

'She's doing another one of them Model
Competitions, in't she? My niece entered it.
Gawgeous, she is...'

Rorie signalled to Elsie; she jerked her head in the
direction of the door to the back room that Miss Multi
had just come from, which was still open. The other

customer had left now; they could sneak out unseen that way, avoiding the glare of the high street. Smooch BB was now playing loud music, which masked any sound they made as they charted their route behind clothes racks and mannequins, over to the back room.

The room consisted of a kitchenette, clothing storage and industrial-style ironing equipment. Rorie led Elsie through it, towards the back door.

But as they reached it, they heard approaching footsteps, followed by a ring on the doorbell. The girls dived behind the nearest clothes rail; sacks of shoes helped provide coverage. Rorie wasn't taking any chances; she covered herself with a fallen coat.

A moment later came the clack-clack of high heels, and the sound of the back door being opened.

'Delivery from Nolita Newbuck,' said a man's voice.

'Oh, yes! *Do* come in!' gushed Estella, suddenly coming over all posh.

'Four racks full,' said the man. 'Where shall I put 'em love?'

'You can bring them straight through to the shop floor,' said Estella. 'We'll go through them right away!'

'No probs,' said the man, and he dragged in the first two racks.

'I must say, Nolita shows the *finest judgment* in selecting this shop for the...further career of her clothing,' wittered Estella as she followed him through.

As soon as it was clear, Roric peeked out from under the coat; Elsie was gone.

The back door flapped; Rorie ran out, and was astonished to see Elsie clambering into the back of the Nolita Newbuck van.

Rorie caught up with her and grabbed her by the trouser leg. 'Elsie, what the heck do you think you're doing?'

'I'm going to get help from Nolita Newbuck,' announced Elsie, yanking her leg away. '*She'll* find Mum and Dad!'

Rorie climbed in after her. 'Are you crazy?' she argued, as she tried to pull her back down the ramp. 'Nolita will just report us to the police, and we'll end up right back at Poker Bute Hall!'

'No she won't!' argued Elsie, wriggling out of her grip.

Rorie glanced nervously behind her, and saw an empty clothing rack emerging from Estella's back door; the driver was coming back for the rest of the clothes.

For now, Rorie had no choice but to follow Elsie further into the van, among some more empty racks. They hid under some blue tarpaulin covers, and seconds later came the clatter of the returning empty racks as they rolled up the ramp. Whistling merrily, the van driver took the second two racks and wheeled them away.

Rorie pulled off the tarp and tugged on Elsie's arm. 'Right, come on!'

'You can't make me,' insisted Elsie, hooking her arm around the steel shaft of the nearest rack.

'Fine!' snapped Rorie. 'You do what you like: I'm going. Goodbye.' Stumbling as she extricated herself from the folds of the tarp, she made as if to leave.

'You don't deserve to have your looks!' called Elsie.

Rorie turned, hands on hips. 'What on earth are you on about now?'

'The *Model Competition*,' growled Elsie. 'Didn't you hear what that lady was saying? You could *win* it, stupid!'

Rorie opened her mouth, ready to spit venom, but nothing more than a croak came out. 'I – oh, don't be ridiculous,' she finally managed. 'I don't want to be a model!'

But there was no chance to argue the matter

further...or to get off the van: the driver was returning for the last time.

Rorie could hardly believe what was happening. Once again, thanks to her *outrageous* little sister, she was forced to get back under the tarp and hide, and this time she would be carted off to Heaven Knew Where, and probably handed over to the police. Only the tiniest glimmer of hope prevented Rorie from giving herself up there and then. She sat hugging her knees, seething with frustration as she sweated under the tarpaulin. She might as well try to carry water in a basket, for all that she stood a chance of controlling Elsie.

The ramp slid inside, and the van doors slammed shut: darkness.

Chapter 24
The Fab World of Nolita Newbuck

A rumbling noise; Rorie awoke. The van was stationary, and the clothes racks were being wheeled out.

Rorie collected her thoughts. She was surprised she'd slept; she supposed she must simply have been exhausted. Outside the van she could hear two men chatting and laughing. Rorie peeked; the driver had his back to them, and his companion was leaning on another rack; this one was loaded with clothes.

'Psst!' She nudged Elsie, who had also fallen asleep.

'Wha? Oh.' Elsie rubbed her eyes.

Not daring to utter a word, Rorie jerked a thumb to indicate that they should leave. She gently slid out from under the tarpaulin on her hands and knees; Elsie followed suit, and the tarp fell quietly away behind them. Rorie peered out between the door hinges; they were in a big garage, at least half-full with vehicles. The driver was still facing the other way, and his friend was now virtually concealed by the clothing rack. The two girls slid down the ramp, and quickly slipped around the side of the van, out of sight. Glancing around, Rorie spotted a doorway. After a few moments, the driver finished his conversation and went back to collecting his racks; the other man wheeled his full rack in the other direction. The two girls grabbed the opportunity and bolted for the door.

The elevator was the sort that runs up the outside of the building, and made entirely of glass. London spread out before them; in one direction the gigantic Helter-Skelter and Cheese Grater towers, the little pointed dome of the Gherkin building poking out alongside them; in the other, the lagoons and bridges of New Venice.

'Cor!' breathed Elsie, her nose pressed against the glass as they sailed upwards.

Rorie gazed in silence.

'You still mad at me?' said Elsie, not taking her eyes off the view.

'I'm not saying anything,' said Rorie.

'You just did.'

'What?'

'Say something.'

'Ha ha,' said Rorie humourlessly.

'What are you going to say to her, then?' asked Elsie.

'Look, I don't know, OK?' snapped Rorie. 'I – just don't know.'

'Might as well try for the model—'

Ding! went the elevator; they had reached their floor. The doors opened to reveal a huge lobby done out in shocking pink, tempered with soft greys. The floor glowed, a moving ripple effect lending the feeling of walking on water. On one wall was a huge screen showing catwalk models dressed in the latest fashions; apparently a sort of Nigerian-Elizabethan look was already taking over from the minimalist Victorian styles worn by the Poker Bute Hall parents earlier that week. Elsie was entranced. A big pink semi-circular reception desk sat in front of a gigantic backlit 3D 'NN'; at the desk sat a slight young man with cropped hair dyed metallic green and violet. 'Can I help you?' he asked.

Rorie opened her mouth, but nothing came out. She had just spotted the name on the young man's identity tag: it said 'Arthur Clark'. 'Um...' she began.

Elsie apparently had not noticed the nametag.

'We've come about the modelling competition,' she piped up, then added helpfully, 'she's the one,' pointing to Rorie. 'I'm too young.'

'You're too *late*, dearie,' corrected Arthur Clark. 'The competition closed yesterday.'

Rorie and Elsie looked at each other. 'Oh, but *please*, sir,' said Elsie, oozing pathos. 'We've come *such* a long way.' Rorie stared at the floor, flaming with embarrassment.

'Oh, unless she's one of the finalists…?' said Arthur, consulting his computer. 'What's the name?'

Rorie grimaced, flummoxed. She hadn't had time to think this through, but she suddenly realised she couldn't use her real name. 'Er…Joyce. Joyce… Harris.'

The young man tapped out the name. 'I don't have a Joyce Harris on the database. What's your entry number?'

There was an awkward pause. 'I, uh, lost it,' Rorie fibbed.

'Tut-tut-tut,' said Arthur. 'Are you *sure* you entered?' He looked them up and down. 'Where are your passes?'

'Um…' Rorie's mouth felt like sandpaper; she cleared her throat. 'Look, I'm really sorry; we thought we could just sort of…show up. I'm sorry to have wasted your time.' Humiliated, she turned to leave, attempting to pull Elsie with her.

'Wait,' said Arthur.

Rorie turned back; Elsie was still rooted to the spot.

The young man leaned back in his seat and studied Rorie curiously, tapping his pen against his lips. 'Darling, you might have made a bit of an effort,' he remarked, a slight mischievous grin spreading across his face. 'I mean, those trousers…they look as if you've slept in them!'

Rorie was so taken aback by his familiar tone, she couldn't prevent a nervous laugh escaping her. 'I…haven't got anything else,' she said, truthfully. She didn't add that she had, in fact, slept in those trousers.

'Hair could do with a bit of a wash, too,' said Arthur. 'Hmm…gorgeous eyes, though. So unusual! Tell you what,' he said, leaning forward conspiratorially. 'Fill out a form and I'll give you a number, OK lovely?' He passed over a clipboard with the form on it. 'Nolita's not seeing the finalists till this afternoon, but if you don't mind waiting…'

'Oh we don't mind!' gushed Elsie, bursting with excitement.

Rorie thanked him, took the form and sat down.

She was just quizzing over her answers (what on earth should she say her address was?) when another girl came in, accompanied by her mother. The girl was decked out in full Nigerian-Elizabethan style, complete with multiple ropes of pearls and some very silly high heels.

Arthur took her details, 'You're ever so early,' he remarked.

'We don't mind waiting,' insisted the mother.

'All right,' sighed Arthur. 'Take a seat.'

Rorie finished with her made-up answers and handed the form in.

'Thanks,' said Arthur. 'There you are,' he added, discreetly slipping forward a number for Rorie to take. 'You'll be seen next.'

'Thank you,' said Rorie. She smiled gratefully at him and took her seat again.

The other girl sneered openly at Rorie's pauper clothing, yet with a slightly insecure air that suggested she felt threatened by Rorie's beauty. She caressed her unfeasibly long, glossy locks, then shot Rorie a challenging look. *Oh, what am I getting myself into?* thought Rorie. Finding it necessary to respond – the girl was staring daggers at her – she ran her fingers through her own hair, then flicked it back in a defiant manner. Elsie copied her moves exactly.

The girl gave them a sarcastic look, winding the pearls around her finger. The necklace broke, sending a cascade of beads to the floor. 'Oh, Mummy!' she cried, and Elsie burst out laughing.

The girl and her mother got down onto the glowing floor and attempted to collect the pearls, the mother scolding the daughter for her clumsiness; Arthur got up to help.

At that moment a door opened opposite, and in walked the lady herself: Nolita Newbuck.

She was a familiar figure to Rorie, known among other things for her weekly digiblog, in which she brought to an eager public all the latest celebrity fashion news, along with her own wit and wisdom on the subject. Women all over the world hung on her every word. Rorie was immediately struck by how small Nolita was; she seemed so big-shouldered and towering on the screen. In fact, although her shoulders were indeed square and muscular, she was merely average in height. But there was absolutely nothing else 'average' about Nolita; she crackled and shimmered like a box of fireworks. Her startling green eyes sparkled with intensity; her big smile flashed with a real diamond. Famously, she never kept the same hairstyle from one day to the next – and frequently changed the colours. Today it was pomegranate red, swept off her face into a tight, high chignon. She strode forth in her mulberry matador suit and high silver boots, talking into her Shel. '...No, hon, it's dull,' she said in that familiar clipped, hoarse New York accent. 'I wanna be set on fire! Think Tashkent, think Samarkand—' she broke off. 'Artie, what happened?' she asked, seeing the mess on the floor.

'Just a small accident, Nolita,' said 'Artie'.

'Call you back,' said Nolita, snapping shut her silver Shel. She frowned. 'The finals aren't till this afternoon.'

'We don't mind waiting,' repeated the girl's mum, grinning obsequiously as she rose up.

'Hmm,' said Nolita. Her eye fell on Rorie and Elsie, and she did a slight double-take. 'You too, huh?'

Rorie felt her face flush; this famous person, this crackling torch of a woman, was actually talking to her! 'Uh...yes, we'll wait,' she managed at last.

Elsie just sat with her jaw hanging open.

'Huh,' said Nolita, and made as if to leave. She paused, and turned to address Rorie once more. 'You know honey, I don't remember you.'

Rorie cleared her throat. 'Um, well...I was dressed

differently last time…?'

The other girl made an unnecessarily loud stifled-laugh sound, and Elsie stuck out her tongue at her.

'No, no, no,' said Nolita. 'That's not it.'

Rorie's stomach began to churn.

Nolita flipped open her Shel again and hit a couple of buttons. 'Yup…gimme ten minutes,' she ordered, then snapped it shut. 'You,' she said, pointing to Rorie. 'Come with me.'

Rorie stood up. 'Um, is it OK if my sister—'

'Yes, yes, her too. Come!' Nolita turned and went back the way she had just come; Rorie and Elsie followed.

Chapter 25
Lipstick and Heels

'Urgh!' groaned Nolita, as soon as they were alone in her rosy-hued office. 'If I see one more girl like that one out there, I shall *scream*, I swear! All lipstick and no smile. *You*, on the other hand...' She looked Rorie up and down, walking around her.

Rorie just stood there, not knowing where to look. In one direction was a vast curved window with a panoramic city view, and Nolita's desk in front of it. More like a sculpture honed from a giant tree than a desk, it had dozens of odd-sized drawers jutting out randomly. All around were sculptures of women's torsos in polished bronze, and at the other end of the room were lipstick-coloured couches shaped like luscious mouths, and a coffee table that looked like nothing more than a piece of translucent draped fabric sitting on thin air.

'What's your name?' asked Nolita, guiding the girls to the seats.

'Ro...Joyce,' said Rorie.

Nolita wrinkled her nose. 'You poor thing.' She glanced at Elsie, who was staring at the video images on the walls of women in wind-blown chiffon, as vivid and delicately defined as oil paintings, yet moving almost imperceptibly slowly. 'You like my office?'

Elsie seemed almost on the verge of tears. 'It's the most beautiful room I've ever seen.'

Nolita chuckled. 'And your name is...?'

'Nikki,' Rorie answered hurriedly, before Elsie had a chance to reply.

Elsie nodded vehemently. 'Yes, *Nikki*.'

'Well, Nikki, welcome,' said Nolita, winking at Elsie. 'Glad you like it. Now, Joyce, I gotta see you in something less ghastly.' She pressed a button on the console beside her, and a pair of double doors slid open. Through them sailed a clothes rail on electronic wheels.

'Wow!' breathed Elsie.

'Sneak preview of next week's styles!' grinned Nolita, flashing her sparkling diamond tooth. 'Take your pick; you can change over there.' She indicated a large, curvy wooden screen nearby. 'Well, go on!'

Rorie stepped forward. She picked the least showy thing she could find – a simple jersey dress – and went behind the screen. She took a deep breath; *stop worrying*, she told herself; *these are brand new clothes*. They had to be, didn't they? All the same, Rorie found it hard to shake the idea that her appearance might change in some unexpected way as soon as she put the dress on.

'Don't forget the shoes,' called Nolita. 'There's a pair in each size.'

'Uh, OK.' Now Rorie felt her insides turn to liquid; the dress might be brand new, but what about the shoes...? Once again she cursed Elsie for steamrollering her into coming here, before she'd had a chance to think things through properly.

Elsie, meanwhile, was ecstatic. 'Oh, Nolita, I think you're amazing, I watch your digiblog whenever I can, although not at...'

Not at Poker Bute Hall, thought Rorie, thankful that Elsie moved on without saying it. She pulled the dress over her head, shaking with nerves as Elsie blithely yammered on to Nolita about how much she *loved* fashion, and *dreamed* of becoming a fashion designer when she grew up. Rorie decided to focus her thoughts on Poker Bute Hall; that would strengthen her resolve. Anything – even the embarrassment of modelling – had to be better than ending up back at that place. She pulled on the high-heeled shoes, praying they were not tainted by anyone else. Well, they *looked* new...

She emerged from behind the screen.

Nolita stood up and strode around her like a circus ringmaster in silver boots, issuing orders with a flourish of her silver-ringed hand: 'Shoulders back! Lo-o-ong strides! Stand tall!'

Rorie did her best to obey the orders, despite her nerves. She glanced at Elsie, who was beaming; *thank heaven*, she thought: she was, apparently, unchanged.

'Now turn!' Nolita went on. 'Hips first, honey... yes?'

Rorie looked round; Artie had appeared in the doorway.

'Can I have a word, Nolita?' he asked.

'Sweetie I'm busy right now, OK?'

'I'm afraid it really can't wait,' insisted Artie.

Then the other contestant's mother barged through, waving her Shel. 'Those girls shouldn't be here!' she yelled. 'They must be turned over to the police at once – look!'

'How dare you come barging into my office!'

retorted Nolita. 'Who do you think you are?'

Artie attempted to restrain the woman. 'Madam, I'm dealing with this; now will you please go and sit down or I will have to ask you to leave.'

'All right,' said the woman reluctantly. 'But they shouldn't be here, I tell you!' she added, wagging her finger.

'Thank you, thank you,' said Artie, closing the door on her.

Rorie and Elsie looked at each other, dismayed.

'Sorry about that,' said Artie. 'The lady picked up a newscast on her Shel. She showed me the pictures.' He turned to Rorie. 'Joyce Harris isn't your real name, is it?'

Rorie sank into the giant lips and felt as if she was about to be swallowed up. 'No,' she admitted, staring at the floor.

For a moment, nobody said a word. Then Elsie burst into a fit of sobs that was extravagantly over-the-top, even by her standards. 'Oh, please don't make us go back!' she wailed. 'We haven't done anything bad, honest, *woo-hoo-hoo*!'

Nolita, meanwhile, had flipped on her screen and was searching the news; in a moment, two huge pictures of Rorie and Elsie were staring back at them, happy simple smiles from back before their lives had been broken. 'Rorie and Elsie Silk, huh?'

The two girls went missing last night from their boarding school, Poker Bute Hall, which is run by their uncle, Mr Harris Silk, went the newscaster's voice.

'Get Mr Silk on the network, Artie,' Nolita instructed.

'Will do,' said Artie, and left the room.

'Oh no, please!' cried Elsie. 'You don't know what he's like!'

Rorie put her arm around her sister. 'Oh Miss Newbuck, we've had a terrible time,' she explained. 'First our parents went missing, and we still don't know if they're alive or dead...that's why we had to stay with our uncle, but he's got some scheme to cut out our inheritance—'

'An' he locked us away in a freezing-cold tower for *weeks* with no food or water!' added Elsie.

'Elsie, don't exaggerate—'

'Well, he would of—'

'Why did he do that?' asked Nolita.

'Because he's wicked!' shrieked Elsie.

'He decided we were trouble,' said Rorie, 'That school...you've never seen anything like it! Everyone's either a P.E. fanatic and a *bully*, or a complete nerd…and they have this motto, *una via rectus*, which means "One Correct Way", and everyone believes this, they think it's wrong ever to do anything differently, *ever*—'

Nolita looked aghast. 'You're kidding!'

'*Really*; they're all like…robots or something, they never question anything, it's…it's spooky!'

'No, stop it!' cried Nolita in mock horror. 'That's terrible!'

'An' they don't let you do any fun things, like drawing or dress-up,' added Elsie. 'An' they make you wear this horrible uniform—'

Nolita shuddered. 'Ugh…bad uniform! Say, what happened to your parents?'

'We don't know,' said Rorie. 'They had a meeting one day, a really important one…but they never got there.'

'They got amneezer,' added Elsie. 'Which means they forgot who they are and where they live, so—'

'Actually we don't know that, Elsie,' said Rorie. 'The police think there may have been an accident, you see, and—'

A trilling sound came from Nolita's desk; she went over and pressed a button. 'Hello? Ah, good, thank you Artie.' Immediately the screen on the wall flickered, and the gigantic head of Uncle Harris appeared. Shaking, Rorie stared, unbelieving; she felt as if her life were folding itself away into a box.

Nolita grimaced at the big, ugly image, and pointed the remote at Uncle Harris to cut him down to lifesize. 'Mr Silk?'

'That's right, yes.'

'I have your nieces here, Rorie and Elsie; I think we need to talk.'

Chapter 26
A No-Brainer

'Mr Silk,' purred Nolita from behind her grand desk, when Artie ushered Uncle Harris into her office. 'Do have a seat.'

'Thank you, but I'll *not* be staying,' snapped Uncle Harris. Rorie was struck by how out of place he looked; like a Brussels sprout in a bowl of bon-bons. He turned to look at Rorie and Elsie, who were sitting on the red-lips couch. 'Come along girls, it's time to go home.'

Nolita stood up. 'Artie? Take Rorie and Elsie for a bite to eat, will you?'

Artie beckoned to the girls and, rather hesitantly, they got up to join him.

'Mr Silk, can we get you anything?' said Nolita politely. 'Tea, coffee?'

Uncle Harris's ears were bright red. '*Miss

Newburgh,' he barked, 'I don't think you heard me correctly—'

'Oh, I heard you just fine, Mr Silk,' interrupted Nolita with a disarming, diamond-glinted smile. 'And I appreciate that you are very busy – so am I. But this needn't take long.'

Then Artie closed the door behind Rorie and Elsie and they heard no more.

An hour later, a pair of burly security men slammed through reception and into Nolita's office, then emerged with Uncle Harris between them. His face was the colour of boiled beetroot – harmonising, Rorie couldn't help noticing, with the shocking pink of his surroundings. 'You'll be hearing from my solicitor about this!' he barked.

'No problem!' replied Nolita coolly.

'That child's wicked, I tell you,' Uncle Harris growled. 'She stole my wife's car!'

Nolita waved this off. 'Come now, you got that back.'

'But she's – she's a witch!'

'And this is the child you are so desperately fond of,' said Nolita, 'that you can't bear to be separated from her; is that right, Mr Silk?'

'A child like that is a danger to society unless she is

thoroughly disciplined,' retorted Uncle Harris. 'You wait; you'll see. You won't know how to handle her!'

Nolita smiled sarcastically as the security men moved him to the door. 'Well, we'll see about that, won't we? Goodbye now!'

Rorie could hardly believe what she was hearing. Uncle Harris paused at the door and turned to Rorie. 'And what have you done with Irmine's jacket, hmm?' he challenged, reaching for her backpack.

The security men took hold of his arms. 'All right, all right, I'm going!' he snapped. 'But the law is on my side – you've not heard the last of this!' And then he was gone.

Nolita came over to join Rorie and Elsie, beaming widely, her diamond-studded tooth glittering. 'Hi. Sorry 'bout that.' She closed the door behind her.

'What did you say to him?' asked Rorie.

'Well, I got the impression you weren't that keen to go back and stay with your uncle,' said Nolita matter-of-factly. She made it sound as if she were talking about a discarded sandwich or something. 'So I figured maybe you could stay with me for a while.'

'Really?' gushed Elsie.

'Sure. Why not? I think it could be kinda fun...don't you?'

'But how…? I mean, won't we *have* to go back to Poker Bute Hall?' asked Rorie.

'I'm a very powerful woman; I generally get my own way,' said Nolita. She beamed broadly, a sudden warmth shining through the cool exterior. 'Artie, what do you think of little Elsie? Isn't she cute?' She pinched Elsie's cheek.

'Irresistible,' agreed Artie.

'And *Rorie*,' said Nolita, slipping an arm around her shoulders.

'So charming!'

'Ah…' sighed Nolita wistfully. 'No one would ever think it, but I get lonely…I do! I've never had the time to get married and have children…oh, think of the fun we could have together!' She clapped her hands excitedly.

Elsie did likewise. 'Yeah!'

Rorie was dumbstruck; she was still amazed that Nolita had made up her mind to take them in so quickly, as effortlessly as other people decided what to have for dinner. She guessed that making big decisions double-quick was what made her so successful. Perhaps this was a good thing, but everything was happening much too fast for her. She had many questions piling up in her head – yet part of her was so overwhelmed with gratitude, she almost didn't care about the details.

Nolita noticed her expression. 'Unless you don't *want* to...?'

'Well, no, I didn't say that,' said Rorie quickly.

'We'd *love* to stay!' said Elsie, brimming over with excitement.

'Ssh, Elsie!' said Rorie. She turned to Nolita. 'I just want to understand this right; *you* could become our legal guardian?'

'OK, here's how it works,' said Nolita. 'We don't really know each other yet. So we have a trial period of, say, six months, see if we get along—'

'Unless Mum'n'Dad come back before that,' Elsie interrupted.

Nolita blinked at her. 'R-i-g-h-t...well, at the end of the six months, if there are no...*problems*...we can then make it permanent. Of course, your uncle will try to get you returned to him. Can't prevent that. But I've laid the groundwork with my lawyers by video conference in there; by the sound of things, he ain't gonna come out of this smelling of roses. So that's the deal.' She stepped forward. 'One thing I gotta tell you right now; I need *complete trust*. You understand? It ain't gonna work if you don't put your faith in me.

That's *real important*, guys.'

Rorie was struck by the intensity of Nolita's stare at that moment. 'Uh…of course.'

'Oh, hey; I hope you're still going to enter my modelling competition?'

'Oh – uh…'

'You do *want* to, don't you Rorie?' asked Nolita, stepping forward. 'You did apply. Or…ah; was that just a means of escape?'

'N-no, it's just…' Rorie hesitated.

'You *have* to, Rorie!' insisted Elsie, hands on hips.

'*OK*,' said Rorie, giving her a fierce look. Then, to Nolita, she said, 'I'm sorry, it's just…I lied about my age.'

'Oh, I knew that,' said Nolita. 'I mean, sure you did! Exactly what I'd have done. So you're not sixteen; what are you, fifteen? Fourteen?'

Rorie bit her lip. 'Twelve.'

'OK, well…hmm, I guess I did think you were a *bit* older, but…what the heck! You can still model the teen stuff. I can get tutors for you both…hey, but any time you want to go back to that boarding school, you've only got to say the word—'

'No!' cried Elsie. 'Never!'

Nolita laughed. 'See what I mean? It's a no-brainer!'

Chapter 27
The Fun Room

The large winter garden on the roof was now swarming with finalists, and Artie was busily organising everyone. 'Need to change, love? Over there, second door on your right...hair and makeup? Booth number four is free...ah, hello Rorie, how do you like the gorgeous dress?'

'Great,' said Rorie, still in a daze. She never usually wore dresses, and this one – very fitted, in smoke-coloured silk and wool – together with the high heels, gave her an unfamiliar but rather thrilling feeling of sophistication. 'Wow, well...I can still hardly believe I'm here, to be honest. Thank you so much for not turning us away.'

'Don't mention it, petal...but relax! You're all tensed up. Enjoy it – it's exciting, isn't it?'

Rorie smiled shyly. 'I guess.'

'*I'm* excited,' said Artie. 'Every year I've been begging Nolita to let me be one of the judges, and finally she's said yes! So of course I'm *insanely* busy...' He peered around the room. 'Any sign of Judge Jenny yet?'

Rorie raised her eyebrows. '*The* Judge Jenny? The one with the net show?'

'Uh-huh, the one and only. She's the other judge today: it's me, Nolita and JJ,' said Artie, still peering around. 'No, doesn't seem to be here yet. Well, sweetie, I hope you're comfortable in that dress. Always a lot of waiting around with these things. Got to go!' He kissed the air beside Rorie's right and left cheeks, then hurried on.

Rorie felt a little nervous giggle escape her. Both Nolita and Artie were more flamboyant than anyone she'd ever met before, and had a curiously familiar air about them, as if they'd known her forever. She wasn't sure how to react, but she knew she liked the warm feeling it gave her inside.

Elsie wiped her mouth with the back of her hand as she finished off yet another chunky caramel cookie from the refreshments table. It was her fifth. She was on her own, Rorie having been ushered off somewhere to rehearse. Watching the finalists get ready for the contest had been completely fascinating for the first few minutes, but people had kept elbowing Elsie out of the way, so eventually she had given up.

Then she'd discovered the refreshments, and had been stuffing herself silly ever since. She washed the cookie down with the remains of her Blue Slush drink, then stuck her tongue out at herself in the mirror, to inspect just how blue it had become; it was satisfyingly lurid. She yawned, and a loud burp bubbled up from inside her. *It's not fair*, she thought, taking another cookie just for something to do. *Why can't I get dolled up as well?* She slid down the wall until she was slumped on the floor.

'Hey,' said a voice. Elsie looked up.

A tall teenage girl was standing over her, smiling. Her platinum blonde hair hung in loose corkscrew tendrils almost to her waist, and she wore a dramatic white and silver dress and black and silver eye makeup. 'How come you're not in the fun room with all the other little brothers and sisters?' she asked.

'Ve fum room?' said Elsie, bits of cookie tumbling from her blue lips. She stood up, finishing her mouthful. 'I didn't know there was a *fun room*!' she gasped.

'Oh,' said the blonde, tossing back her tumbling locks. 'Well there is; I know 'cause my little brother's there. Um...' She glanced at the time. 'I could probably show you where it is...I'm just waiting around right now.'

'Ye-eah!' said Elsie, and she eagerly took the girl's outstretched hand and went with her out of the studio and into the elevator.

'Try to *relax*, Rorie,' said Tinky, a young assistant with a winning smile who was coaching the aspiring models on their moves. 'You're hunching your shoulders, like you want to hide away in your shell! OK, go and practice...next!'

I'm no good at this, thought Rorie despondently as she stepped down from the catwalk. *And why should I be? I've been forced into it by my little sister, of all people!* Rorie felt conflicting emotions; on the one hand, she was grateful to Elsie for the way things had turned out. But on the other hand, the whole modelling thing just felt embarrassing. She really didn't want to do it now; she felt sure she would trip up in her high heels, or something.

She sighed. Where was Elsie, anyway? She had last seen her at the refreshments' table, so she went there;

no Elsie.

Rorie went to the toilets. 'Elsie?' she called out to the row of locked cubicles. Nothing. She turned to leave, and was halfway out of the door when a tall blonde girl in a white and silver dress emerged from one of the cubicles.

'Are you looking for someone?' asked the girl.

Rorie turned back. 'Oh, yes – my little sister.' Something about the girl seemed vaguely familiar, but she couldn't quite place her.

The girl pushed her hands into the cleanse unit. 'What's she look like?'

'Uh, she's about so high,' – Rorie indicated with her hand – 'mousey hair…wearing a sort of funky outfit with a skirt and leggings…'

'Oh…just saw a girl like that leave with her dad a minute ago,' said the girl, removing her hands and teasing her platinum locks with her fingers.

'Her *dad*?' gasped Rorie. She felt her heart fall through the floor. 'No – th-that had…had to be some other girl.'

The girl paused and blinked at Rorie through her heavy black and silver makeup. What *was* it about that face?

'Oh…well, maybe you should ask at the desk,' she

suggested, glancing sideways at herself and smoothing down the fabric of her dress. She headed for the door.

'Uh, excuse me?' said Rorie, following the girl. 'Where did they go, this girl and her, uh—' She began to get a nasty prickly sensation all over.

'Don't know,' said the girl. 'Why don't you call?'

'Oh. I can't. The, uh, dad – what did he look like? Was the girl happy, or – or not?'

The girl smiled. 'Oh, she was *fine* – that's why I noticed her. Laughing and skipping...didn't really see the dad. I don't know where they were going, but she took her sweater – a green thinfat?'

It has *to be her*, thought Rorie.

She went to consult Artie; she found him surrounded by a group of finalists. 'Artie?'

'Just a moment, Rorie,' he called without looking up, holding up his pen. 'Number twenty-one...Elysia?' he said, addressing one of the finalists. 'Are you done with grooming? To the green room please, and do *not* leave...'

Rorie waited for a moment, then repeated, 'Artie!' more forcefully...but there was so much noise, he didn't hear. Rorie looked for Nolita, but couldn't even find her. She could wait no longer: she headed for the main door, leading out to the hall, and called the elevator.

Laughing and skipping, she thought to herself as she descended in the elevator. She tried to be reassured by this, telling herself it couldn't possibly be Uncle Harris stealing her away if she was laughing and skipping – and besides, security would never have let him in. No: there was no way it was Uncle Harris. And Rorie didn't dare allow herself to wonder if Dad had returned. That *really* didn't make sense: he would have come looking for her too!

Which only left…Rorie felt a hard lump in the pit of her stomach. It would be *so* like Elsie to wander off with a complete stranger if she was getting bored. She had a way of bonding instantly with people; getting so carried away with her tall tales, she would forget everything her parents or school teachers had ever told her about not talking to strangers. Feeling ever more panic-stricken and confused, Rorie descended to the lower ground floor and emerged into the car park.

'Rorie!' came Elsie's voice, echoing around the gloomy concrete walls. It was a sharp, hoarse cry.

Rorie searched wildly. 'Elsie?' She dashed between the rows of cars, but the cry was not repeated. Then there was a muffled thudding sound, and Rorie saw: Elsie was in Uncle Harris's car, thumping on the now closed window – and there, in the driver's seat, was Uncle Harris.

Rorie propelled herself towards the car. The high heels made her twist her ankle: she threw them off. Still Elsie thumped, and Rorie heard her muffled cries. Reaching the car, she pulled on the handle of the rear door. It opened. Elsie, having been leaning heavily on the door, fell towards her. Rorie caught her with her right arm, but just as she reached in with her left to gain a secure grasp of her, she felt a violent shove on her back, and she was forced forward onto the seat of the car, rolling over Elsie. Amid the screams and chaos, Rorie heard a *clunk*!

'Well done, Nicola,' said Uncle Harris. 'Excellent work.'

Rorie looked up: there, in the passenger seat, was the platinum-blonde girl from the ladies' room. In the tussle, her hair had fallen to one side of her head, so that from the angle Rorie was seeing her, it was all swept off her face. In spite of the heavy make-up, the way her cheeks were now flushed with colour made Rorie suddenly realise who she was.

'Nikki Deeds!'

The champion athlete had apparently sprinted down the thirty-one flights of steps at incredible speed, and got to the basement before Rorie.

Nikki strapped herself in. 'Belt up – if you want to stay alive!'

Both Rorie and Elsie made futile attempts to open the locked doors. Elsie, who was behind Nikki, lunged at her, screeching like a wildcat; meanwhile Rorie, grabbing the opportunity caused by this distraction, slid her hand towards the door-locking-control on the door next to Uncle Harris.

Within seconds both attempts were foiled, as Nikki overpowered Elsie, and Uncle Harris wrested Rorie's hand away...now both Uncle Harris and Nikki Deeds were wearing pollution filter masks, and Nikki's hand came forward – a flash of something metallic and a hissing sound, then a fragrant mist...Rorie found her vision going blurry...

'That's better,' said a hollow voice she guessed belonged to Uncle Harris. There was a vague sensation of movement now. Roric slumped in her seat; Elsie did the same.

'You can't do this,' Rorie tried to protest – though it came out more like 'you carnndothishh...' Elsie was now sound asleep; Rorie fought it. Her arms and legs felt like lead, and her mouth felt almost as if it had ceased to communicate with her brain.

Uncle Harris drove off. 'It's for your own good,' came his echoing voice. 'It's just a mild sedative.'

Summoning all her strength, Rorie replied, 'you can't force uss ter...stay wiv you if we don' wannoo...'

'Ah, but that's just it,' said Uncle Harris, pulling off his mask. 'Very soon you *will* want to. In twenty-four hours, with a little anger management training, you'll see things differently.'

Rorie struggled to stay conscious, but she was sinking fast. Uncle Harris' words turned bendy, reverberating around the inside of her skull. *Twenty-four hours...anger management...see things differently...*

Now the words 'Anger Management Course' hovered in her head, bringing with them images of Moll...Frumpy-clothed, bright-eyed, ponytailed Moll, saying *it's amazing how a bit of time away can change how you feel about things.* Inside Rorie was screaming *no, no!* but she had sunk into a horrible dream, and no matter how hard she tried to cry out, she was voiceless.

Chapter 28
The Necklace

'*Aaaaurgh!*'

The guttural, bone-tingling scream launched Rorie back to consciousness with an almighty surge. She sat up abruptly.

It took her a while to gather her senses. The first thing she realised was that she was in Uncle Harris's car; the second was that Aunt Irmine had somehow acquired long blue hair. The third thing Rorie realised was that it wasn't Aunt Irmine sitting next to Uncle Harris, but Nikki Deeds – and her hair was a strange colour because it was covered in blue vomit.

'Eurgh! My hair!' shrieked Nikki, utterly horror-stricken.

Rorie turned and saw a very green-faced Elsie sitting bolt upright, remarkably free of blue vomit herself, save for a small dribble on her chin. She had apparently aimed spectacularly well.

Uncle Harris, still driving, turned and grimaced – only to be on the receiving end of a second generous helping of chunky-caramel-cookie-and-Blue-Slush-flavoured projectile vomit right smack bang in his face. 'Guh!' was all he could say, his face constricted with disgust as glutinous blue blobs slid down his face and dangled from his nose and moustache.

The car swerved; a loud horn sounded. 'Pull over, *please* Mr Silk!' cried Nikki Deeds. 'I can't find any tissues...I really need to clean up!' she warbled, frantically searching various storage compartments in the car.

'Right,' said tight-lipped Uncle Harris, straightening out the car.

Rorie still felt a little woozy, but everything was coming back to her now and she was aware enough to sense that an unmissable opportunity might be fast approaching. She looked over at Elsie. 'Are you 'kay?' she asked drunkenly.

Elsie just stared blankly ahead. Usually she bounced back all sparkly after a good upchuck, but this time she was, unsurprisingly, more subdued. Still, Rorie was reassured to note that she seemed purged and calm. As Uncle Harris and Nikki Deeds argued over where they would stop – they were currently on a motorway – Rorie suddenly had another thought; that she and Elsie had better pretend to fall back to sleep if they didn't want to get another cloud of sleep-mist in their faces. If that happened, they hadn't a hope in hell of getting away. She slumped back, and nudged at Elsie's foot to prompt her to do the same. Eventually Elsie understood, and she too assumed the rag doll pose – though Rorie worried that their captors might not be convinced by the scrunched-shut eyes.

'...There isn't another fuel station for twenty kilometres,' Uncle Harris was saying.

'Oh, sir, I know where we are!' cried Nikki. 'Please sir, we're near the reservoir...that bridge...that's where the canal is. We could pull over here...'

'The *canal*?'

Nikki's voice was desperately shrill. '*Please*, sir!'

'All right, all right,' said Uncle Harris. Rorie felt the car slow down and stop. Uncle Harris's voice grew slightly louder as he apparently turned to glance at his passengers. 'I'll lock 'em in. Come on.'

A rush of cool air and white noise as doors were opened. *Clunk, clunk*...then a third, soft *ker-lunk* that Rorie recognised as the sound of the central locking system being engaged.

She waited.

Elsie stirred. 'What're we—'

'Shh!' Rorie peered out of the window to see if they were free to move. Uncle Harris and Nikki were some twenty metres away, disappearing down a grassy bank; soon they'd be out of sight altogether, as was the canal. Rorie hoisted up the skirts of her luxurious dress – which, she was relieved to note, seemed to have escaped any vomit-spattering – jumped into the driver's seat, and strapped herself in.

'You gonna drive away?' asked Elsie.

'Gonna try,' muttered Rorie, hitting the 'ID override' button. 'Now,' she said, shaking her head in an effort to overcome her sleepiness, 'I juss need to remember that code – ah, what *was* it?'

Elsie looked out of the window. 'We better be quick.'

'Yes! All right!' replied Rorie testily as she stared at the keypad. 'Look, just...don't talk.' Spotting a half-drunk shrink-pack of Scarlet Ram Hyper-Energy Drink in the console – Nikki's, judging from the lipstick marks on the straw – Rorie grabbed it and gulped down what was left, in a desperate effort to perk herself up.

'Rorie,' said Elsie.

'I said *don't*—'

'Yeah but—'

Rorie, held up her hand 'Tssht!'

'It'snotAuntIrmine'scar!' Elsie blurted as quickly as she could, before Rorie could interrupt again.

'I know that!' squeaked Rorie. 'Look, they're bound to use the same code as each other, just like Mum and Dad – ah! That's it! Six-two-seven-nine…I'm *sure* of it.' The Scarlet Ram already seemed to be having some effect.

She tapped in the number: *Code invalid*, said the car. *Please try again.*

'Oh no,' sighed Rorie. 'You know what? They've changed it, because I stole Aunt Irmine's car – man, what was I thinking? Of *course* they'd do that!'

'If only we had Aunt Irmine's jacket now,' said Elsie despondently.

Rorie frowned. 'I don't even know how that works. I mean, would she have had to wear it again…? Oh good grief, we're wasting time.' She banged her fist on her forehead. 'What else could it be? It could be anything!' Her brain was nothing but fog.

'If Moll was here, she'd know probably,' said Elsie.

'What do you mean?'

'She told me she figured out the codes on the school

locks...oh, hey! Does your changing magic work with joolery as well as cloves?'

'Why?'

Elsie pulled out the silver orchid necklace from inside her shirt. 'I forgot I still had this on,' she said, taking it off and handing it to Rorie. 'It's Moll's; she lended it me, an' I was gonna give it back but I din't get a chance, and then...'

Rorie grabbed it eagerly. 'It's hers? She actually *wore* it?'

'Yes.'

Rorie quickly put the necklace on. 'You say she figured out the codes?'

'Yeah, but she wouldn't tell me how.' Elsie sat forward, leaning on the back of the seat in front of her. 'Hey, d'you think this'll really work?'

'It's all we've got,' said Rorie, gazing anxiously out of the window. *But the transformation might take too long,* she thought. She yanked hard several times on the door handle. 'You know, I swear you're supposed to be able to get out of a locked car in an emergency...I guess Uncle Harris has thought of that. He must have set it so that it wouldn't.' She tried a different approach: waving her arms around frantically at the cars and trucks as they whizzed by on the motorway. 'Oh, it's no good; they're going too fast to notice anything.'

Elsie, meanwhile, was thinking of Uncle Harris and Nikki Deeds 'They're gonna be back any minute,' she said, glancing towards the canal.

Rorie didn't respond; she just stared at the keypad, concentrating for all she was worth.

Elsie moved closer and peered at her. 'I fink you're shrinking,' she whispered.

Rorie, too, was aware that her dress was feeling looser. But she didn't waste time looking in the mirror, just went on staring at the keypad. She felt a glimmer of an answer...then nothing. She took a deep breath, looked away, then stared again. Now she felt the familiar sensation of something else taking over. 'It's almost certainly the same as the school lock codes,' she found herself saying. 'There are four different codes, one for each wing; Poker, Bute, Tzikan and Friesan. But' – she scrunched her eyes tight, and her words flowed faster – 'they're all combinations of the same four digits...One Cor-Rect Way, O-C-R-W, or six-two-seven-nine – that's the one I did! So: one down, three to go...OK, let's try, nine-two-seven-six.' She tapped out the numbers as she said them.

Code invalid, announced the car dispassionately.

You have one more attempt. Vehicle immobilisation will occur upon third incorrect attempt.

'Oh no!' cried Elsie.

'Right: there are two more school codes,' said Rorie-Moll, sweat breaking out on her forehead.

'...But you've only got one go,' Elsie pointed out, helpfully.

'I *know*.'

'Choose one!' cried Elsie, jumping up and down. 'I *see* them, Rorie – they're coming back!'

'Oh! OK, I'm just gonna...here goes.' She tapped in 2, 7, 9, 6...

Beep. *Thank you*, said the car. *Hmm*, went the engine.

Rorie immediately slammed her foot on the accelerator and whooshed into the nearside lane – only narrowly missing another car.

Chapter 29
Rebel Spirit

'OK,' said Rorie. 'This is OK now, Else. Don't worry, I'm in control.'

'I'm scared!' cried Elsie. 'You don't know how to drive!'

'Yeah, well, but…right now all I have to do is keep going in a straight line.'

'What about when we're off the motorway?'

Secretly, Rorie was worried about this too, and she held the steering wheel in a fierce grip. Her mouth was parched. 'Oh, it won't be hard,' she assured Elsie in the breeziest manner she could muster. 'I mean, I can sort of remember how to do it from when I was in Aunt Irmine's jacket.' She paused. 'Oh boy.'

'What?'

'We need to turn round; we're going the wrong way.'

'Oh yeah.'

'But we can't – we'll be caught in no time. Uncle Harris is bound to be onto the police by now.'

'Oh.'

Rorie just kept on going for several kilometres; she had no option. When she felt confident enough to take a hand off the wheel, she removed Moll's necklace, so that she could transform back into herself; her little Moll legs had to stretch right out to reach the pedals. Elsie took the necklace and put it back around her own neck.

Then they came to an exit; Rorie took it.

'What you gonna do now?' asked Elsie.

Rorie slammed on the brakes, suddenly realising she was approaching a roundabout much too fast. The car veered sideways as it skidded to a halt past the dotted line. *Honk, honk!* went several other cars. Now Rorie was gripped with fear; that brief little jaunt in Aunt Irmine's jacket had been scant preparation for the present situation. 'Oh!' she wailed. But she pressed on determined, easing out as soon as the way was clear, following the direction of all the other vehicles. It was a large roundabout with at least six exits, as far as Rorie could tell. Because she had no idea which one to take, and because she was almost paralysed with fear about making any decision at all, she just kept on going round and round.

After the fourth circuit, Elsie said, 'We can't stay here forever, Rorie. Can't we do the navigation thingy?'

'No, I can't set the destination yet,' said Rorie. 'I'd need to stop, and…oh, here goes.' She made a turn, opting for the one which wasn't the motorway, but looked as if it was heading roughly the right way. She was instantly assaulted by another barrage of honks and hoots.

'The blinker!' cried Elsie. 'You're meant to use the blinker!'

'But I don't know where—' Rorie tried moving one lever; the windscreen wipers came on. Seeing a car approaching them from the side, she braked again; then, stopping and starting, alternately setting off the wipers and the screen wash, she eventually made it to the exit.

'OK, stay calm,' said Rorie, taking a deep breath now they were back on a straight road. 'It'll be fine now, I promise.'

Elsie, meanwhile, was practically hyperventilating in the back seat. 'I wanna go home!' she wailed.

Arriving at a traffic light, Rorie tried to set the

navigation system. 'Oh.'

'What?'

'We don't actually know where Nolita's headquarters are, do we? I mean, we got there stowed away in the back of a van, and we left asleep.'

'Well it's in *London*,' said Elsie simply.

'Yeah, Elsie, London's a big place!' The light changed; she had to go.

Now what? Rorie asked herself. She had no idea, so she just kept going straight. That, at least, was relatively easy. And perhaps eventually there would be a sign for New Venice, which she knew was near to Nolita's; if she could get close, she might see the building and be able to figure out the rest of the way...

Moments later came the last sound in the world she wanted to hear: a police siren. And it was getting louder fast. This time, Rorie felt sure they were after her; she stepped on the accelerator. In the rear-view mirror, she could see the flashing blue light approaching. Frustrated with the speed of the car in front, she overtook on the wrong side; before she knew what she was doing, she was weaving in and out of the traffic, hurtling along at breakneck speed. The numbness in her head made the whole thing feel slightly unreal, as if it wasn't actually happening to her...and perhaps it wasn't, quite. She felt as if something of Moll's rebel spirit was inspiring her, even though she had now, she reckoned, fully transformed back into herself. She was playing the part of Bad Girl – and it felt exhilarating.

Elsie bounced around in the back, yelling, 'Faster, Rorie, I see them!'

Weeyaw weeyaw! The police car was fast advancing; meanwhile Rorie was stuck behind two lorries side-by-side, with no way round.

Police, pull over, came an amplified voice. *Pull over immediately.*

Rorie felt the sweat trickle down the side of her face as she contemplated squeezing in between the two lorries. For a moment, the gap between them widened, and she surged forward, leaning on her horn, but the gap closed again, and a booming horn blared. She retreated, and the Zedforce car advanced alongside her. *Pull over to the r—good lord; the girl is driving!*

Rorie was so surprised to hear this, she turned and looked. Sitting in the passenger seat of the police car, and talking into the PA system, was Inspector Dixon.

Pull over to the right, he repeated, but this time he added: *don't worry, I'm taking you back to Miss Newbuck.*

Chapter 30
Shocking Pink

Inspector Dixon, it turned out, had been assigned the task of tracking Rorie and Elsie down, as he had already been working on the girls' disappearance from Poker Bute Hall.

'Now, Rorie,' he said, as they sped towards London, 'you do know it's an offence for a minor to drive a vehicle on the highway?'

'She's not a miner!' Elsie piped up.

The driver chuckled.

'She's under seventeen,' explained Dixon. 'And presumably inexperienced. Twice now! *Very* dangerous – to others as well as yourselves.'

Rorie stared at the floor. 'Yes, I know.' *But I* wasn't *inexperienced the first time!* she was desperate to say. *I was being Aunt Irmine!* But of course she couldn't say that – and Elsie, for once, had the sense not to either. Besides, it didn't excuse this latest jaunt.

The detective sucked pensively on his butterscotch sweet. 'Hmm, well…there are, of course, other factors to take into account. Stress, anxiety…'

'Is there any news about Mum'n'Dad?' asked Elsie.

'Actually, I tried to reach the excavation people this morning,' said Dixon. 'They were expecting to finish any day now. But a communications mast was destroyed along with the tunnel, so we may have to wait until the end of the day. There have been no sightings reported, I'm afraid. Now, perhaps you can fill me in on exactly what happened this afternoon?'

Elsie explained how Nikki had conned her into following her to the basement, where she was bundled into Uncle Harris's car, and Roric told of the way Nikki had then lured her down as well.

'Yes, apparently she got in by impersonating a genuine contestant,' remarked Dixon.

Something else now drifted into Rorie's mind, as it continued to clear from the sedative: Uncle Harris saying they would soon change their minds about returning to Poker Bute Hall. Had he really said that, or had she dreamt it? But what had happened with Moll hadn't been a dream. What exactly would she tell Inspector Dixon about that, though? That Moll had been dressed differently? Differently from what – her school uniform? That she *seemed* different – when she hardly knew her anyway? What was he supposed to make of that?

Besides, Dixon had moved on. 'Your uncle clearly won't accept the arrangement with Miss Newbuck. Are there any other family members who can support your case?'

'Well, there's Great-Grandma,' said Rorie, doubtfully.

'But she's Too Far Gone,' added Elsie.

'Elsie! What she means,' explained Rorie, 'is that she's 112 years old, and in an old people's home.'

Inspector Dixon took out his Shel. 'Well, give me the details anyway; you never know.'

'Well, well. I knew you were shy, honey,' quipped Nolita, when at last they returned. 'But I didn't think you'd go to quite such lengths to get out of being in the contest!'

Everybody laughed, and Rorie laughed along with them, so relieved was she to be back. Surprised as she was, she felt grateful to Nolita for making light of the situation; she didn't think she could have handled a big drama.

'OK. Does this mean we can go ahead with the show?' said a short, stocky black woman with a tall copper-coloured hairdo, who Rorie recognised instantly as Judge Jenny. 'My backside went to sleep about three weeks ago, and I'm ready to follow it to the land of nod.'

'Of course,' said Nolita, who today wore her hair in large, sculpted curls, the red complementing the shimmering sea green of her glamorous evening jacket. 'Tinky? A new outfit for Rorie, please!'

'Miss Newbuck,' said Inspector Dixon. 'I need to speak with you in private.'

'Sure, of course!' said Nolita. 'But we really must go ahead with the contest now; you will of course be staying until after it's finished? Really, there's no telling *what* might happen next around here!'

'You have a point, Ma'am,' nodded Dixon.

The girls followed Tink into the changing room. 'I can hardly believe everyone hung around and waited for me!' said Rorie, as she slipped into the new, vivid pink dress. She felt more conspicuous than ever, and positively dreaded going out in front of everyone.

'Rorie's in trouble for stealing cars!' Elsie told Tink.

'All right, Elsie,' said Rorie.

'She's a criminal,' Elsie went on.

'Elsie!'

'Here, don't you worry 'bout that,' insisted Tink, as she applied Rorie's lipstick. 'The way that uncle of yours 'as behaved? *Tut tut*; good for you, for gettin' away, I say!'

Elsie admired the dress. 'That's the pinkest pink I ever saw.'

'That's why it's called "shocking pink",' said Tink. 'All right, missus,' she said, turning to Rorie. 'You're done. Now, none of this shoulders-hunched business. Go on out there and knock 'em dead!'

Amazingly, Rorie suddenly felt as if she wanted very much to do just that. She wondered if this was down to the chameleon effect; had she somehow absorbed the shocking pinkness, the hey-everybody-look-at-me-ness of the dress? She was glad to note that her *skin* hadn't turned pink. But this *was* the first time since the lightning incident that she had worn anything remotely colourful...

Stepping out onto the catwalk, Rorie held her head high.

Chapter 31
Scary Tall Hair

The air was thick with anticipation, as the winners were about to be announced. Some of the finalists toyed with their drinking straws, pretending not to hope it would be them. Others wore the skeleton-grin of the desperate, imagining they merely looked pleased for others.

By now Rorie was staring at the glass roof and the sky beyond, her mind somewhere else entirely. The sensation she had experienced out there in the pink dress had reminded her of something Dad had once said, when she had asked him how on earth he managed to stick with his work, to keep on trying, even when his experiments went wrong. 'The first step is believing you can do it,' he had said. Suddenly those words took on a new meaning for her, right here and now. She realised that this had been a first step for her;

she had *believed* she could go out there and not trip up, not make a complete fool of herself. It may not have been half as daring as somersaulting out of a tower window, or zooming off in a car – but the difference this time was that she wasn't hiding behind someone else's identity. And all it had taken was a pink dress. Then thinking of Dad had set her off on a familiar cycle of anxious thoughts about where Mum and Dad were now...She was so preoccupied, she didn't even hear the announcement at first.

'...And the winner in the Young Teen category is... Rorie Silk!'

Rorie went on staring at the ceiling. Elsie nudged her. 'Rorie! You won a prize!'

'Wha...? No!' said Rorie, sitting up abruptly. 'It *can't* be me...'

'It is!' insisted Tinky. 'Go on! Go up and get your trophy!'

'I knew she'd win,' said Elsie. 'I just knew it!'

Rorie did as she was told, and stepped up into the blaze of lights.

There was a commotion in the audience. Someone was pushing their way through to the front, pursued by a security guard.

'What is going on?' demanded Nolita, then, 'Oh,

not you again!'

'You don't have the right to take those girls from their home!' yelled Uncle Harris.

'I'm sorry madam,' said the security guard. 'I tried to make him wait...'

Nolita groaned. 'Oh! Kill the cameras, guys, we're pretty much done here anyhow...Mr Silk, you are the most ghastly bore I think I've ever met. I thought we went over this already; *you* posed a risk to the children, *we* got a protection order...By the way, shouldn't you have been arrested by now? You're not allowed to steal them back, you know.'

She turned to Inspector Dixon, who duly stepped forward – with some relish, Rorie thought. 'Harris Silk, I arrest you on the charge of unlawfully removing children from their home.'

'Ah, but you see she didn't have the grounds to take them away in the first place,' pronounced Uncle Harris, holding up a small rectangular e-document. 'I have here an injunction, and I'll prove it in court; the girls may *claim* they were at risk – but I can prove otherwise!'

'Whoa, whoa!' called Judge Jenny, angrily smacking the desk in front of her. 'This fella's not for real! OK, now let's get this straight, and let's do it quick, before I get bum-ache again. You, sir; you forcibly removed these girls, young Rorie and her sister, from their new residence. Yet you say you pose no risk to them? Why should anyone believe you?'

'Who is this woman?' said Uncle Harris disdainfully. 'I don't have to answer to you, Madam.'

Judge Jenny stood up, hands on hips; almost a third of her overall height was made up of that scary copper hair. 'Oh, I think you better had, sir.'

'She is in fact a Q.C., Mr Silk – a highly respected judge,' Inspector Dixon informed Uncle Harris, whose expression instantly changed from indignant scowl to ingratiating simper. 'Your Honour; I did not, in fact, *forcibly* remove them.'

'Ooh, what a lie!' shrieked Elsie. Laughter broke out all across the room, and Uncle Harris was confronted with a sea of faces, all challenging him to refute the charge.

'All right!' yelled Uncle Harris. 'That's enough; Miss Newbuck, I'll see you in a *proper* court, after this has gone thorough the *correct* procedures. I am now entitled to remove the girls.'

'You are entitled to nothing of the sort, I can tell you right now,' said Judge Jenny. 'You can take the matter to court, and you can argue your case, and for all I know you might win that case...'

Rorie shuddered at the thought.

'...But as things stand, sir,' Judge Jenny went on, 'the girls legally reside with Miss Newbuck.'

'And I do actually have to take you to the station now, sir,' Inspector Dixon reminded him.

'Oh yes; this may well involve a prison sentence,' added Judge Judy, wagging a pointy copper-coloured nail at him.

Uncle Harris was silent for a moment, as he contemplated this. Then his head lowered, and his face took on an awful sort of puppy-dog expression. 'I only did it because I love my nieces so much!' he wailed.

Rorie and Elsie looked at each other, dumbstruck.

'I'm so distressed about my missing brother,' Uncle Harris went on, 'He wouldn't want his daughters living with a perfect stranger; I know he wouldn't! The girls are all I have right now!' he pleaded. 'Your Honour, Miss Newbuck, I apologise unreservedly for my actions; I temporarily allowed myself to believe that...that *love* was all that mattered. I'm just... terribly upset.'

'He's not upset about Dad at all!' yelled Rorie, rather taken aback by her own forcefulness. *It must be the pink,* she thought. *Well, pink it up for all you're worth,* she told herself; there was a battle to be won here. For all of Nolita's reassurances about her powerful team of lawyers, Rorie was troubled by Judge Jenny's words about the possibility of Uncle Harris winning his court case. There must be *no* chance of that. 'He doesn't even *like* our dad!' Rorie added.

'Yeah, and our dad doesn't like him!' said Elsie.

Now for the big one: Great-Grandma's will. Rorie didn't have any proof about that, but she had to give it a go all the same. 'The only reason Uncle Harris wants us with him,' she blurted out, 'is because he thinks it would make our great-grandma change her will in his favour!'

Pink attack! Uncle Harris's sweaty face was pink and shocked. 'That's a blatant lie!' he protested.

'Oh, is it?' said a voice at the back of the room. Everyone turned: there, at the entrance, sat an extraordinary vision in white and grey, three attendants in tow; Great-Grandma herself. She waved a gnarled hand, and the nurse behind her wheeled her forward, until she was lit up by a spotlight. 'Well!' said Great-Grandma. 'Isn't this nice?'

There were a few murmurs, then Great-Grandma signalled she was ready to speak again. 'Now then, I don't get out a great deal, but it so happens I've been having some of these new-fangled rejuvenating treatments – don't I look fabulous?'

She certainly did look a good deal livelier and healthier than when Rorie had seen her last. Uncle Harris looked on in disbelief.

Nolita introduced herself. 'And you are...the girls' great-grandmother? I gotta say, your timing is incredible.'

'Isn't it just? Ooh, I've not felt this well in *years*,' said Great-Grandma. She turned fiercely to Uncle Harris. 'And I'm not planning on popping off any time soon, y'know!' she snapped. 'Now,' she went on, addressing everyone else. 'Good heavens, what a day it's been! First I hear that my great-grandaughters are on the loose. Then I get a call from the nice policeman, saying they're all right, but would I come and make a statement? *Well...*' She paused to clear her throat, then take a sip of the water offered to her by one of her nurses. 'And here I am!' She gazed at the audience. 'My, there are a lot of people here, aren't there? Why don't you talk amongst yourselves for a while?' She waved a hand at them, then turned to Rorie and Elsie. 'Now, my dears; I dare say that with all the charging about, you've not heard the latest news.'

Rorie felt her heart surge. 'What news?'

'Well, it's not what you or I were hoping,' said Great-Grandma. 'But on the way up here I saw a piece of breaking news about some excavation work that was going on, at the site of a collapsed bridge?'

'Yes?' said Rorie and Elsie together.

'Well, it's finished.' Great-Grandma's eyes drooped.

The girls waited in vain for more. 'And?' They turned to Inspector Dixon, but he was only now checking the situation and not ready to report back.

A nurse prodded Great-Grandma, and she jolted awake. 'Oh, did I nod off?'

'Yes,' murmured the nurse.

'Ah, well,' said Great-Grandma, folding her hands and gazing around her. 'Is it tea-time yet?'

The nurse whispered something in her ear.

'Oh! Right,' said Great-Grandma. 'Sorry. These rejuvenation things, you know...they may make you look and feel twenty years younger, but that still makes me like a ninety-two-year-old. Now then: the excavation. You see, they didn't find anything.'

'Nothing?' said Rorie.

'Not. A. Sausage,' said Great-Grandma. 'Not even a car. Nothing; zip. So you see,' – here she turned defiantly to Uncle Harris again – 'Arran's still out there, you know; somewhere! *And* young Lorna...er, Laura? *Laura.*'

Uncle Harris's upper lip twisted into a sneer – but he stopped short of saying anything.

Not even a car, thought Rorie. Her heart did a somersault. Not until this moment had she realised how much she had been filled with dread about that excavation, every day expecting to hear that something had been found. Next to having Mum and Dad come back, this was the best possible news.

'Well, this is all very fascinating,' said Judge Jenny to Great-Grandma, 'but perhaps you can clear something up for us, madam. Did your grandson, here – Harris, is it? Yes? Did Harris try to make you change your will in his favour, on the basis that the two girls were residing with him?'

Great-Grandma's watery blue eyes sparkled with anger. 'Yes!' she proclaimed.

The entire room full of people – who had most certainly not been talking amongst themselves – gave a collective sigh.

'Thank you,' said Judge Jenny. 'I think that clears things up very nicely.'

Uncle Harris's face, which had been tensing itself up more and more during the whole exchange, fell apart.

His eyes searched wildly, as if trying to find some way to wriggle out of this, but it was hopeless. His nasty little scheme was public knowledge now, and there was nothing he could do about it.

'I think it's time we headed down to the station now, don't you, sir?' said Inspector Dixon, laying a hand firmly on Uncle Harris's shoulder.

'He always was thoroughly unpleasant,' Great-Grandma pronounced loudly. 'Used to smash up things his brother made – molecular models and so forth. Yes!' she croaked angrily at him as he shuffled past, head hung in shame. 'Don't think I've forgotten about that!'

Chapter 32
Big, Beautiful Butterfly

All was quiet. Everyone had gone home, and the cleaner bots were busy clearing up. Clean-faced and back in her own shabby clothes that were like a second skin, Rorie felt wonderfully ordinary again; invisible. She picked up her backpack and checked its contents: Aunt Irmine's jacket, Leesa Simms' cravat, Nikki Deeds' smelly trainers…boy, she would need to get those washed. For a moment she wondered if that would spoil the effect – then she remembered Caroline's shirt, fresh from the laundry; that had worked, hadn't it? What a mysterious business it all was. Then there was Moll's necklace, safely hanging around Elsie's neck. Four people whose expertise she could call upon, should she need to. She couldn't think right now of any situation in which she *might* need them…but she would hold onto them anyway.

'Are we ready to go then, girls?' said Nolita, appearing at last in a simple black trouser suit, her hair scraped off her face.

Elsie slid off her seat, a happy, droopy-eyed smile on her face and threw her arms around her.

Nolita laughed and put an arm around each of them. 'Well, ain't this exciting? And you, my new Young Teen Model, Rorie. How about that? No, let's not discuss that now. You've had an exhausting day!'

Elsie's face took on a faraway look. 'Nolita?'

'Yes?'

'Will you help us find our Mum'n'Dad?'

Nolita patted her on the head. 'Sure!'

'I mean, with your great big team of lawyers, an' everything; should be easy, right?'

'Elsie, it's not like they can magic them out of thin air, you know,' said Rorie.

'It's OK,' said Nolita. 'We got you away from your beastly uncle; I can see why Elsie might think there was something magical about that!'

'Thank you so much, Nolita,' said Rorie. The words seemed inadequate somehow, but she didn't know what else to say.

'Hey, you don't have to keep thanking me!' said Nolita. 'I never did anything I didn't want to do. In bald commercial terms, hon; I find a rare bloom like you, it's in my interest to put you in my hothouse. Ain't the first time one of my models has stayed with me; you're just the youngest, that's all. And as for Elsie here; I'm sure gonna enjoy having her around!'

Elsie beamed up at her, bursting with admiration.

That night, Rorie had a dream about shoes. She was in Nolita's office, standing behind the screen, and an electric shoe rack wheeled its way over to her. On it was a solitary, gigantic pair of shoes. Rorie stood and stared at them. They were easily one and a half times her own height, and from heel to toe they were about the length of a rowing boat.

'Go ahead and put them on,' came Nolita's voice from the other side of the screen.

'But they're way too big,' said Rorie.

'Nonsense!' said Nolita. 'They'll fit you; just give it a try.'

'You have to try, Rorie,' came Elsie's voice. 'You *have* to.'

All of a sudden, Rorie had a sense that getting into these shoes was a matter of life and death. This was something she must do.

She hoisted herself up one of the shoes, using the

huge platform sole for a foothold. She clambered in, then stood up and placed one foot in the other shoe. Whether the shoes shrank or she expanded was not clear, but in an instant, Rorie found that Nolita was right; incredible as it might seem, the shoes did fit her. She tried to walk, but they weighed her down like a ton of lead.

'I can't move,' said Rorie. 'They're too heavy.'

'Keep trying,' came Nolita's voice – only it wasn't Nolita's voice any more; it was Dad's. 'Keep going,' he said, 'don't ever give up.'

'But it's so hard.' Now she was out on the Hammerball pitch in the wind and the rain in the big heavy shoes. 'And I don't understand the rules of the game.'

'You've got to *try*,' said Dad, whose face, along with Mum's, appeared on a screen attached to a moving goal.

'Yes, you've got to,' added Mum. 'Don't worry if they think you're crazy.'

Rorie tried, but the shoes were still so heavy, and the goal was moving, and still she didn't understand the rules of the game.

The goal disappeared into the distance. The rain stopped, and the wind died down. Sunlight glistened on the raindrops. Elsie appeared beside her, and a big, beautiful butterfly flew past, saying, 'The first step is believing you can do it.'

Elsie went skipping after the butterfly. And slowly, slowly, Rorie picked up first one, then the other lead-heavy shoe, and began to follow.

Have you read the *Lulu Baker Trilogy*
by Fiona Dunbar

The
Truth
Cookie

*Discover a magical recipe book that
gives Lulu Baker the power to change lives...*

Lulu's dad has a new love, Varaminta le Bone. She's
a sizzling sensation...and pure poison. How can Lulu
make her dad see Varaminta, and her odious son
Torquil, for who they really are?

Then Lulu stumbles into an odd little bookshop and
Ambrosia May's mysterious recipe book falls at her
feet. *The Apple Star,* together with some *very* unusual
ingredients, just might do the trick...

Cupid Cakes

Thanks to Lulu Baker and her magical recipe book, The Apple Star, romance is in the air!

Lulu and her best friend Frenchy are inspired by the school production of *A Midsummer Night's Dream* to play cupid to Lulu's dad and...Frenchy's mum!
But no sooner has Lulu whipped up the recipe for Cupid Cakes, and given Dad a taster – disaster strikes. It soon seems like everyone is falling in love with the wrong person!

And there is something deeper and darker worrying Lulu. Evil Varaminta le Bone and her tricksy son Torquil are back! Varaminta has uncovered the magical powers of *The Apple Star* and now she'll stop at nothing to get her hands on the book...

Imagine a magical recipe to make all your dreams come true!

As Lulu scales new heigths with her enchanted recipe book, she discovers that the evil Varaminta is looming again – and this time she has joined forces with an international arch villain! Lulu faces her greatest challenge yet...Will she be rendered powerless or can she overcome them to gain a happy ending?

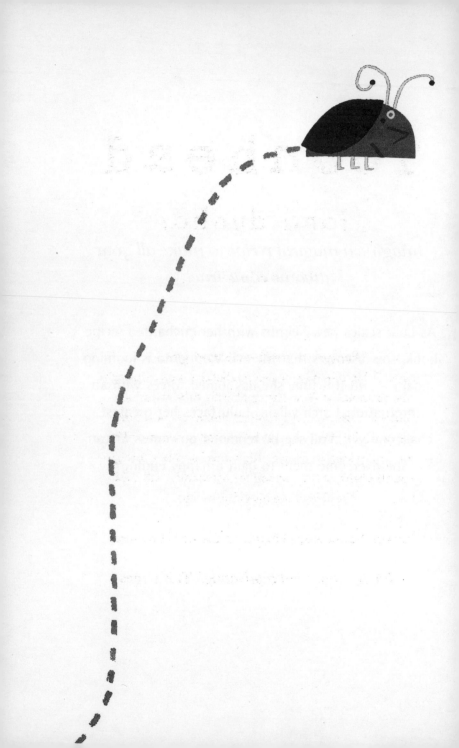

Toonhead

fiona dunbar

978 1 84616 238 1

£5.99

Pablo has a gift – a secret gift.
When Pablo discovers he can predict the future through
the cartoons he draws, he can hardly believe his luck.
But what seems to be a brilliant discovery soon turns
into a terrible burden, as Pablo's secret is discovered by
the wrong kind of people. Kidnapped and in a foreign
country, with only a cartoon for company – will Pablo
be able to use his gift to escape?

Expect the unexpected in this off-the-wall adventure.

"Fresh, Funny and captivating." The Times

*Turn the page to see more
Orchard Books you might enjoy...*

Do Not READ This Book

As revealed only to Pat Moon

978 1 84121 435 1

£4.99

WARNING!

Snoopers watch out!
Fierce guard-bunny on patrol!
So paws off this book!
That includes my friend, Cassie. And
especially MUM. Who's FAR too busy
drooling over creepy-crawly Action Man to
care about what I think anyway.

Shortlisted for the Sheffield Children's Book Award

Utterly M
Clarice Be

By Lauren
Child

978 1 84362 304 5

£4.99 (utterly worth it)

This is me, Clarice Bean.
Mrs Wilberton, my teacher, wants us to do
a book project – which sounds utterly dreary... until I
find out there is an actual prize. Me and my utterly
best friend, Betty Moody, really want to win...but how?

'An utterly fantastic book.' The Sunday Times

'Very entertaining.' The Independent

'Feisty and free-wheeling. Hilarious and
irresistible.' The Financial Times

Other Orchard Books you might enjoy

Clarice Bean Spells Trouble	Lauren Child	978 1 84362 858 3*
The Truth Cookie	Fiona Dunbar	978 1 84362 549 0*
Cupid Cakes	Fiona Dunbar	978 1 84362 688 6
Chocolate Wishes	Fiona Dunbar	978 1 84362 689 3*
Clair de Lune	Cassandra Golds	978 1 84362 926 9
The Truth about Josie Green	Belinda Hollyer	978 1 84362 885 9
Hothouse Flower	Rose Impey	978 1 84616 215 2
My Scary Fairy Godmother	Rose Impey	978 1 84362 683 1
Shooting Star	Rose Impey	978 1 84362 560 5
Forever Family	Gill Lobel	978 1 84616 211 4*
Seventeen Times as High as the Moon	Livi Michael	978 1 84362 726 5
Do Not Read – Or Else	Pat Moon	978 1 84616 082 0

All priced at £4.99 except those marked * which are £5.99

Orchard Red Apples are available from all good bookshops,
or can be ordered direct from the publisher:
Orchard Books, PO BOX 29, Douglas IM99 1BQ
Credit card orders please telephone 01624 836000
or fax 01624 837033
or visit our Internet site: www.wattspub.co.uk
or e-mail: bookshop@enterprise.net for details.

To order please quote title, author and ISBN
and your full name and address.
Cheques and postal orders should be made payable to 'Bookpost plc.'
Postage and packing is FREE within the UK
(overseas customers should add £1.00 per book).

Prices and availability are subject to change.